BOBBI BLUE

A TRUE STORY OF LOVE & TRUST

HEATHER LAMONT

Sunny Ville
P U B L I S H I N G

Bobbi Blue
A True Story of Love and Trust
by Heather Lamont
Copyright © 2021 Heather Lamont

ALL RIGHTS RESERVED

Layout & graphic design by ED&M Design
background by K.J. Pargeter

First printing: October, 2021

ISBN: 978-0-9975658-7-4

Printed in the United States of America

This book is dedicated to my Father God

whose perfect love casts out my fears.

Endorsements

WOW! Loved what we managed to read together so far. What a fabulous idea to write a children's book using real life stories and photos of Bobbi Blue's experience of overcoming fear. A delight to read with my 10-year-old daughter who loves horses and has herself overcome scary things. We decided Bobbi Blue was an inspiration.

—Karen Scott (Mum of three)

Daughter Abi says:

I love these stories of Bobbi Blue. I loved hearing about the things he was afraid of and how his mum helped him realise there was no need to be afraid. I love horses so the real photos were really good. I'd love to meet Bobbi Blue some day.

HEATHER (Bobbi Blue's mum) has sensitively woven together experiences with her beloved pony into a beautifully written collection of short stories, addressing fears and challenges that parents and teachers can explore with their children.

These heartwarming yet reassuring stories draw the reader into the world of adventures Bobbi Blue and Mum face as they grow together in confidence, love and trust. Heather has given a treasure trove of stories, creatively threaded with spiritual truths, that not only will delight but offer precious times for sharing.

Bobbi Blue's escapades are an invaluable resource, ideal for parents to use in discussion and for teachers to use during circle time in the classroom.

— Beryl Johnston (teacher)

TO BOBBI BLUE, I wish I could hug you! Thank you for leading us from fear to faith! Please tell your mum (Heather) that I absolutely love these pony parables, and already see how both children and adults (myself included) are benefiting from the indescribable peace that comes from trusting in God!

—Leila Grandemange (Author, "Pawz and Pray")

A FANTASTIC READ full of excellent lessons which have been put across in a way that children can relate to. The author's ability to highlight simple problems that life can throw at us, with engaging stories about the famous Bobbi, is impressive and heartwarming. Knowing the connection Heather has with her horse and knowing the level of truth behind the stories, adds authenticity.

—Donal McKinley (manager/owner of Shean's Horse Farm.)

Contents

Acknowledgements

Thank you to my friends Margaret and Doreen for all their help, encouragement, constructive suggestions and generosity which enabled me to write this book.

Special thanks to my dear friend Leila. Her help in producing this book was absolutely invaluable and I will be forever grateful.

Thanks must also go to MaryAnn who edited my book with great patience, laid it out and designed the cover.

Thank you to Shean's Horse Farm for all the fun and enjoyment we found there and of course for letting us bring Bobbi Blue home!

I'm so thankful for my faithful husband Rob who has done so much of the practical work with Bobbi Blue. He has seen very little of me in recent months as I have been either riding or writing!

Helpful Tips
for adults reading this book with a child

🎗 Create a pleasant, loving environment where the child can relax and read independently or with a family member. This could be curled up on the sofa with you, at the kitchen table or in their bedroom.

🎗 Manage reading time. Although each chapter is designed as a short story, the topics on fear may not be suitable bedtime reading for younger children.

🎗 Make sure the child is not too tired to converse as discussion is very important. It might be a good idea to read through the stories yourself first. Reading time should be pleasurable so try to avoid interrupting other things your child finds enjoyable.

🎗 Praise the child constantly whether they are reading aloud or quietly by themselves and encourage their comments, listening intently.

BEFORE READING:

🎗 Discuss the front cover and what the title might convey.

🎗 Ask the children to imagine things Bobbi Blue might be afraid of. This should give insight into their fears and emotions.

🎗 Talk about the chapter titles and photographs.

AFTER READING:

🎗 Talk about each chapter. Encourage the child to retell the story in their own words, describing what Bobbi Blue was afraid of and why he should not have worried.

🎗 Give the child opportunity to discuss their own emotions. Did they have a favourite story and why? Have they ever felt like Bobbi Blue? Who could the child talk to if they are worried or afraid? What do they think trust means? Could the child give Bobbi Blue any more advice for the future?

1
Bobbi is Afraid

Bobbi was a little pony who had just come to live on a horse farm with many other horses and he was scared of EVERYTHING! Mud stuck to his thick winter coat and although he wasn't cold, he shivered constantly because he was so afraid. He had grown up wild and free but sadly the farmer who owned him had sold him.

Reluctantly he had been taken away from his first home and now he found himself surrounded by both people he did not know and large ferocious-looking horses. Bobbi was so traumatised he wondered . . . what horrible thing was going to happen to him next?

But he soon discovered that he should not have worried about the people at all. They were full of fun and more than kind to him. A gentle lady called Grace noticed him looking afraid. She stroked him and petted him and tried to calm him down. After a little while a man called Ben broke Bobbi in and taught him all the things a pony needs to know so that he could be ridden. To Bobbi's surprise, he enjoyed this experience and afterwards had a good long rest in green pastures. However, life still wasn't happy.

The people at the horse farm had been so kind to him. Bobbi relaxed when his human friends were around as they were so much fun and he felt safe. But Bobbi still had a big problem.

He had been right to worry about the other horses! They were mean to him when they were on their own. They made him stand back from the food until they had eaten the best of it. They bit him and kicked out at him and even pulled his mane out in mouthfuls. Big Blue was friendly to him, but this was not much help at feeding time. The bigger horses wouldn't let Bobbi sleep with them in the big shed so poor Bobbi had to lie in the mud outside in the cold and dark. He was so lonely and afraid. Over time Bobbi learned how to stand up for himself better, but now he longed for someone to love him and protect him.

One day a lady he had never met before appeared. She seemed to recognise that Bobbi was looking for a relationship with someone who was not his own kind. She looked at this sad little pony shivering on his own with his head down and asked Ben if she could ride on him. "Yes," said Ben. "He is my favourite. He is so kind, gentle and keen to learn."

So, Bobbi and the lady set off up the mountain to places Bobbi had never been before. That's where the love story began. Little did he know that this lady was the mum he had been looking for all his life. Could her love help him conquer his fears? Over time Bobbi became more and more submissive and obedient in response to her love. He began to believe this lady called Heather could be trusted. Bobbi got a new name—Bobbi Blue, as Heather discovered when she groomed him that he was a beautiful blue and white colour under the mud. The colour blue is connected to royalty and is associated with trustworthiness and reliability. His name was often shortened to Bobbi but he knew he had been given a very regal title.

Bobbi Blue watched and waited expectantly every day for the lady arriving with treats, which he had never known before. Bobbi decided he would call this lady Mum as she silenced all his fears when she was with him. But Mum didn't come every day, so Bobbi Blue called after her when she disappeared each time. Why did she have to leave? Where was she going? What if she didn't come back? Bobbi felt so alone, he held his head low and trembled.

He was very afraid.

2
Bobbi and the Bags

Bobbi Blue should not have worried. Mum was never going to forget about him. In fact, Mum would visit him at the horse farm almost every day for four months. Bobbi loved to be out and about on the mountain at the horse farm with his Mum. However, there was something which terrified him, especially in stormy weather—plastic bags!

Mum had said, "Trust me," but it was very hard to trust her when faced with these horrors. Bobbi Blue always kept an eye out for them, even when there was no sign of them. He knew his Mum loved him. But one morning when Mum collected Bobbi from the field where he was happily munching grass, she did a terrible thing to him.

Bobbi walked happily into the stables expecting to be groomed but (Shock! Horror!) he was surrounded by the things he dreaded most, for his stable now contained huge bags, hanging from the ceiling, which swept over Bobbi's back menacingly as he tried to escape. How could the Mum he had begun to trust do this to him?

It seemed like Bobbi had been put in a prison. At first, he was climbing the walls. Locked in and surrounded by things which made him so fearful, there was no avoiding them, no opportunity to run away. It's so awful to feel trapped when you don't understand what's happening. Mum talked soothingly and gave him his favourite tit bits. She stroked him and brushed him (which he loved), underneath one of these fearsome objects.  Each day he made progress as he relaxed in Mum's presence and gradually realised that actually there was nothing to be afraid of.

Sometimes those things which terrify us are totally harmless and we have just imagined the horrors; they aren't real. Mum would never intentionally harm Bobbi Blue. Yes, the bags were still there, but they weren't going to steal his joy. He learned to just ignore them. Mum explained she hated seeing him imagining things that might never happen. It broke her heart watching him closed in with his fears, but she knew it was for his good. And she said it seemed that, somehow, she loved him even more when he was scared and miserable. Mum was so proud of Bobbi's progress in conquering his irrational fears and soon they would enjoy a fear-free mountain top experience together. Bobbi would never fear bags again. He had faced this fear and was more than a conqueror! All things had worked together for good.

Bobbi Blue, however, was beginning to worry about something else: "What if the birds flew out of the trees suddenly? What if they landed on him? What if..." Mum stopped him and said quite firmly, "No more what ifs! Those are bad words. Do you think the birds are worrying?"

Mum had a Big Word Book which she loved. She quoted from it: "Refuse to

worry about tomorrow, but deal with each challenge that comes your way, one day at a time. Tomorrow will take care of itself."
—Matthew 6:34 TPT

3
Fear of the New!

Mum was very proud of Bobbi Blue's new found courage to overcome his fear of plastic bags. It had been very stormy but Bobbi had become accustomed to his familiar route and walked sedately past plastic bags flapping dramatically in the wind. Occasionally a bird flew out of bushes unexpectedly and made Bobbi jump. He quickly realised however that his fear of birds was also unfounded, they couldn't hurt him.

Bobbi became quite relaxed in his familiar surroundings and was happy unless something changed. He was afraid of new things, they made him feel very insecure.

New fears for Bobbi Blue were still lurking around every corner. One day Mum and he set off on their ride round the horse farm. They had just turned around the first bend, when (Shock! Horror!) Bobbi discovered a large pile of very strange, intimidating obstacles which had never been there before. What could these things be? They looked very sharp and threatening. Were they going to attack him?

Bobbi Blue hated new things. He wanted to know what was going to happen every minute of the day. He didn't want anything to change. His immediate reaction to these fencing posts (for that is all they were) was to turn and run in the opposite direction but Mum firmly and gently turned him back towards them. There was no going back!

Mum said there was no insurmountable object that they couldn't face together. Besides, this was just a pile of logs. She assured Bobbi Blue in a gentle voice that the new things were constructive and to be used for good for the other horses and himself. They would make protective fences. Mum encouraged him and whispered, "I am with you, do not be afraid. I will help you."

Well, Bobbi had learned to trust Mum more and more, and listen to her voice, especially when she quoted from her Big

Word Book. So, although he didn't like it, he very cautiously walked past these dreaded apparitions, then back and forwards with his confidence growing on every approach. To Mum's delight they were able to fearlessly approach these new, inanimate objects and pose proudly beside them for a photograph. Well, maybe he had a little flick back of the ears at them! Bobbi was gradually overcoming his fear of new things.

"It's a journey," said Mum. "Never forget we are in this together." She quoted from her Big Word Book: "Be strong and courageous. Do not be afraid or terrified for the Lord your God goes with you; He will never leave you nor forsake you." —Deuteronomy 31:6 NIV

Mum was feeling positive and pleased with Bobbi Blue, but what was round the next corner?

4
The Song

Bobbi Blue still hesitated as birds suddenly fluttered out of hedges but soon gained his composure again. He was becoming accustomed to riding out around the mountain with Mum and he had fewer things to fear each day. Now he was at the stage where he could bravely ride out with a group of other horses and lead the way. But trouble was waiting for them one day.

All of a sudden, the horses in neighbouring fields started galloping furiously, very close to the group of riders. The riders were becoming quite frantic as their horses bucked and prepared to gallop alongside and the riders wondered what to do. Should they dismount voluntarily? Then an experienced person suggested that they start to sing a song to calm the horses and so they began to sing a chorus of "Jingle Bells." Bobbi Blue thought that to be quite ludicrous in the month of February! Mum didn't know the words of "Jingle Bells" and had already been singing "Jesus, How Lovely You Are," knowing how that calmed both Bobbi Blue and herself.

Mum was so proud of Bobbi Blue who now led the others calmly past the stampede and down the hill to safety. He is such a sensitive pony, that he felt peace when Mum called on the name of Jesus. She would sing in days to come when ugly fears arose and trust faltered, "Jesus, name above all names, what a powerful name it is," and Bobbi relaxed in the calm embrace he felt through Mum.

You will have realised by now that Bobbi Blue is a very smart pony. He quickly added the name Jesus to his growing repertoire of words: "walk on, trot, whoa, steady, wait, back."

Oh, wait a minute! He was throwing out the word "back." He hated having to walk backwards. There was no going back for Bobbi Blue!

5
Bobbi Learns about Discipline

Bobbi Blue had a wonderful day. The sun was shining so he, Mum, Dad, and his friend Big Blue rode to the top of the mountain and enjoyed glorious views. It was thirsty work but the rivers were so refreshing and he drank long and deep. When they came back down Dad and Big Blue headed home to the other horses for a rest.

But oh, the disappointment! it seemed Bobbi was being separated from his friends and had to continue on his own around the bottom of

the hill. Bobbi wanted to be with the other horses. He was scared to be alone or to do anything they weren't doing. He didn't want to be different.

Bobbi was so anxious that he became angry and started to misbehave. He soon expressed his displeasure by shaking his head, stamping his feet and crunching on his bit. Mum ignored his displays of annoyance and carried on at a very slow and boring walk! At long last they came to the home stretch again.

Bobbi was bursting with anticipation at the thought of seeing his friends and his food again! He was just about ready to explode into a billion horsey pieces. It was decision time—fight or flight. Fighting against Mum hadn't worked, so Bobbi chose the flight route! He determined to run off. He took off like a race horse out of the starting gate! Well, his excitement was soon curtailed when Mum shouted, "Whoa!" and pulled him into the hedge to stop.

Did she call him names and remind him that he was a cob, not a thoroughbred? Did she accuse him of acting like a bull? Did she smack him with her whip? No, Mum didn't condemn or

accuse Bobbi Blue, although she did discipline him because she loved him so much. She didn't want Bobbi to act in fear like this, so she scolded him and told him he was naughty. She had pulled him into the hedge so that he would be safe; going too fast up that stony hill would damage his feet. There are some harmful things in life which you should have a healthy fear of. Mum explained she has to discipline the one she loves. She would have to chastise him because he was hers and she wanted the best for him.

Bobbi had to learn to be obedient and submissive, for his own good. Running away from things that make you anxious is not a good idea. So, they walked round that hill at Mum's pace three more times until Bobbi was relaxed and co-operative!

Mum was so happy that Bobbi Blue allowed himself to be disciplined. She told him that they might get some dressage lessons in future so that they could learn to dance together as one. That would be something they could both look forward to. Meanwhile, they met some other riders and Bobbi Blue was allowed to follow them around and chill. In fact, they stopped and Mum treated him to a graze on the new sweet grass along the banks with the other horses. He was glad he didn't miss that.

Soon he was back home with Big Blue tucking into a hearty feed. This had turned out to be a fantastic day and Bobbi Blue was looking forward to his next training session. Mum always knows best.

6
Bobbi Submits

Do you ever feel fed up? Wish everybody would leave you alone? That you would like to hide from scary things all day rather than face them? That you don't want to go anywhere? That's how Bobbi felt one day.

Mum was late coming to visit and he had decided to roll in the mud, then sleep under his favourite tree. He just wanted peace and quiet, to do his own thing; but no, here was Mum, bridle in hand, ready for action. She tacked him up and decided to do some training. Bobbi dragged his feet and if he could have, he would have rolled his eyes and said, "Not today!" Mum, however, wanted to do a recap of some things he had learned. At first Bobbi was a bit concerned and wondered if Mum really loved him. She trained and disciplined him quite regularly. Bobbi Blue, however, was learning not to be afraid of this quite continual discipline, although sometimes he felt he'd had enough of it.

Bobbi reluctantly decided to cooperate, but to show his displeasure he gave two bucks as he passed his tree. Well (Shock! Horror!) Mum gave him two sharp smacks, scolded him and insisted he canter on. She made him train harder, riding him in boring circle after boring circle and over countless poles on the ground! Why did she do this to him? How could she?

Mum said, "Don't lose heart." She was doing this because she loved him?! Really?! Bobbi was hers. If she didn't discipline him, it would show that she didn't care how he turned out in future, and nobody likes a spoiled little pony. The discipline wasn't pleasant; in fact it was painful, but it just lasted a short time.

Bobbi submitted and was gaining more respect for Mum. He had to realise that he didn't know everything but because Mum was in control, he had no need to fear. He accepted that Mum is boss and he is not. Bobbi felt not so afraid when he handed control over to Mum. Her ways are best. And her treats afterwards are the best too! They took a little scenic walk and Bobbi Blue finished the morning feeling super fit and very content. He nuzzled up to Mum and was rewarded with lots of carrots and cuddles.

Bobbi had to learn respect for Mum. He had to learn when he wanted things his own way to say, "Yet not my will, but your will be done." Mum could be trusted to protect him when he stayed within her boundaries. Bobbi Blue knew he would be safe in Mum's care every day, no matter how he was feeling.

7
Bobbi Gets Sick

Bobbi Blue wasn't having a good week. He had picked up a cold virus and just wasn't his usual energetic self. Mum had to stop riding him and forced him to rest. He felt so sick and miserable, in fact he felt horrible. His nose was running, he had a bad cough and a very sore patch on his skin. He missed his canters full charge to the mountain top but he just felt like sleeping. Life was now boring and monotonous. Could it get worse?

Yes. In order to prevent the spread of the virus, the decision was made to isolate him from the

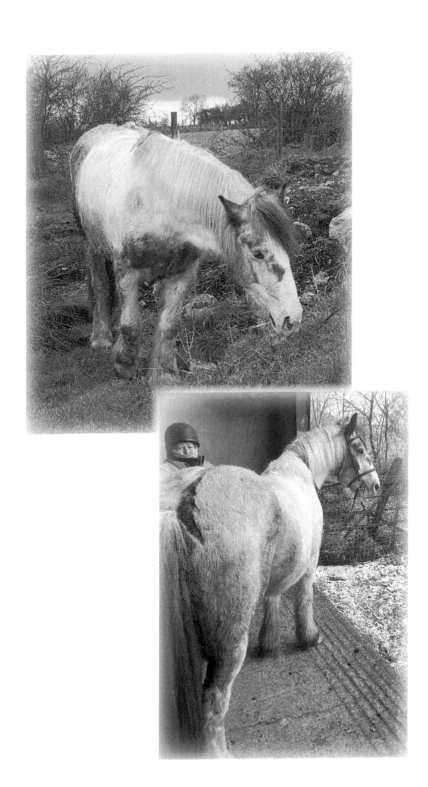

other horses including Big Blue. They called to each other from a distance but that just wasn't the same. Mum seemed to understand this was for everyone's good to prevent spread of the virus, but Bobbi certainly didn't understand. He hadn't chosen self-isolation; it had been forced on him.

Then horror of horrors! Men came and stuck needles in him. They were so painful, though admittedly he did make more drama out of it than necessary. Mum said these injections would make him feel better but Bobbi was afraid that this would happen to him every day.

Poor Bobbi was traumatised. He had no idea why Mum would allow this to happen to him. What had he done to deserve this? He had been so good recently. Mum and Dad visited regularly and pampered him, but were upset when he hid from them in fear. Bobbi worried and had some horror-filled thoughts—what were they going to do to him next? Why was this happening to him? When would he feel joyful again?

But little did Bobbi know what Mum had planned for him. She had never wanted this to happen and she apparently wasn't by his side all the time for a reason. Even when Bobbi couldn't see it, Mum was working, making a way through this. She would use this as good preparation for a glorious future she had planned for Bobbi Blue. You see, Mum was preparing a place for him. A very special place. Although Mum had often hummed the song, Bobbi didn't know the words, "Way Maker, Miracle Worker, Promise

Keeper, Light in the darkness, my God, that is who you are."

Oh no! Mum and Dad have just packed Bobbi into a horse box and headed on a long journey. What is happening now?

8
Bobbi Arrives Home!

Although it was only 30 miles from the horse farm to Mum's home, the journey had seemed long to Bobbi Blue. But now he had arrived at his final destination—Moorfields! Mum had been very busy preparing a special new home for him. She explained that she had paid the price for him and he was now hers, that Bobbi would live with her from now on . . .

Mum explained he had walked through a dark valley but now those horrible days were behind him. Nobody would ever bully him again. Bobbi felt so much better now that Mum and Dad had brought him to be with them and that this would be his forever home. They promised that Bobbi Blue would lie in green pastures. He would lack nothing. There was nothing for him to fear for they would always be with him.

Mum read from her Big Word Book: "Surely your goodness and love will follow me all the days of my life." —Psalm 23:6 NIV

The door of the horse box opened wide, Bobbi heard horses whinnying in the distance, a gurgling stream and a chorus of birds singing. The smell of sweet grass filled his nostrils.

Bobbi cautiously stepped out into this fascinating place and was escorted to his accommodation. He was delighted firstly to use his ensuite sleeping quarters and have a quick nibble of fresh haylage. He was then shown to green pastures and told he could run free. Run? No. Roll in the deep sticky mud? Oh yes!

Bobbi was in heaven! Heaven is a place on earth! Then he began to worry. Was this too good to be true? Bobbi Blue figured he should stay in a corner in case he got into trouble and would be sent away.

9
Bobbi Settles In

obbi was still dubious when turned into the huge field. Mum had laid out certain boundaries to keep him safe but Bobbi still had acres of new sweet grass to devour. Mum removed his head collar and expected him to gallop off joyously as most horses would. But no, Bobbi immediately put his head down and frantically started munching on the odd blades of old grass in the mud at the gate. He had got used to other horses allowing him their leftovers. Bobbi was content to potter among the weeds and rubbish because he didn't expect anything more. He stayed close to the clothes line, hoping to get reassurance from Mum's clothes when she wasn't beside him. (He also added his lovely horsey odour to the clothes in case Mum would forget him!) He had no idea of the abundance that had been provided for him as part of his new family. Bobbi Blue had never seen or heard of such a huge expanse for one little pony. It was too much for his mind to conceive and his tummy to receive!

Go, Bobbi Blue, don't be afraid, raise your head, raise your expectations and enjoy limitlessness. . .

Bobbi gradually gained confidence and began to enjoy the abundance that was his. He ventured further through his pastures, enjoying the beauty of the rivers, lakes and blossoming flowers. But then he allowed the old doubts and fears to creep in: was he good enough to deserve this? Would Mum remove all his pleasures if he misbehaved? Would she still love him if he was naughty?

Bobbi decided to test this out!

Where would he start? Oh yes, Mum's beloved cherry tree on the other side of the fence! It didn't taste great but Bobbi chewed it down to a stump. Would he be banished from the fields? No, Mum simply put a barrier up and said it was to prevent Bobbi getting sick. Bobbi then tried to reverse into the fence and knock the barrier down. Mum certainly didn't praise him, but did she stop loving him? No, she laughed and told everyone how smart he was.

It seemed he could do no wrong in Mum's eyes; he would have to give her one more test. Mum seemed to love that ridiculous clothes line. She spent soo much time at it. Bobbi devised a cunning plan to test her love. He decided to demolish the beloved object. He gripped it with his teeth and flung it down the field as far as he could! If Mum could forgive this, it would be clear that her love was genuine.

Well, Mum's grace was amazing. She shook her head incredulously but again she laughed. And laughed. Bobbi Blue began to realise that he was deeply loved and his reaction to this love could only be gratitude. So, he promptly decided to help Dad fix the precious clothes line. Bobbi's supervision was invaluable! He loved to supervise all Mum and Dad's activities. Bobbi was realising that just being in their presence was allaying many of his fears but he had more to learn . . .

10
The Shelter

Bobbi Blue still had a bit of a cold and the weather at Moorfields had turned nasty. Rain, sleet, hail, and strong biting winds blew around Bobbi's paddock. Mum wanted Bobbi to stay warm and dry in the storms in order to speed his recovery. However, Bobbi Blue had his own ideas. He liked to stand at the gate where he could survey the traffic or entice the occasional unsuspecting passer-by to give him titbits. "There will be nobody out walking in that storm, Bobbi! There is no shelter from that miserable tree." Mum often said.

When the hail and rain lashed very heavily, he sheltered under the remains of his favourite sparse pine tree. There was no protection there. He stared down at the shelter which Mum and Dad had carefully prepared for him, but unless they were there enticing him with a carrot, he had no intention of going in. For once again Bobbi was afraid! He was terrified of every rain drop that hit the tin roof. What a noise they made: "pitter patter, pitter patter."

"Come on, Bobbi Blue," said Mum. "This is a refuge from the storm. It is a safe, warm place with plenty of clean bedding to relax on and fresh haylage to indulge yourself on. Why won't you take shelter in the storm? You would heal so much faster. . ." Bobbi was not going to admit his horror of this "safe place." He would have to be introduced to it gradually, not all fears are overcome quickly.

It seemed that Mum knew how he was feeling and would faithfully leave food and fresh water for him every day in that safe shelter, no matter what the weather was like. The shelter would always be there, when Bobbi was ready to use it.

Mum read Bobbi Blue some comforting words from her Big Word Book. "God, you're such a safe and powerful place to find refuge! You're a proven help in time of trouble—more than enough and always available whenever I need you." —Psalms 46:1 TPT

"He offers a resting place for me in his luxurious

love. His tracks take me to an oasis of peace,
the quiet brook of bliss." —Psalms 23:2 TPT

11
The Monsters

Bobbi Blue was getting used to his new surroundings. He loved playing with his new doggy friends and kind horse neighbours Julie and Poppy. The green pastures, the still waters, which refreshed Bobbi, were so peaceful.

One Spring day he and Mum were enjoying climbing the hill path to get a view over the local countryside at Moorfields. There were some obstacles on the path or alongside it. Bobbi passed branches, streams, sheep trotting alongside, animal feeders. Together they chased the crows away. No obstacle deterred Bobbi Blue now that he was becoming braver. That is, until they came upon the monsters!

Lined alongside the lane, was a group of hairy, very strange-looking objects. Bobbi wondered if they were monsters who had come from another planet. They seemed to be bubbling out of the ground as if they were preparing to erupt. In fact, they were just piles of straw, but Bobbi Blue began to imagine all the horrors that could befall him if he passed these monstrosities. But Mum was insisting that he walk on. He didn't want to. Why did Mum not get rid of these objects of terror? Or take him a different route to avoid them? She seemed really very harsh with Bobbi Blue. She told him that some things don't shift on this earth, so you have to learn not to fear them.

Especially when your fear is unfounded. Mum reminded Bobbi quite firmly that she was with him, speaking the name Jesus and squeezing him tightly with her legs. Before Bobbi knew it, they were past those fearsome obstacles and it was a distant memory!

The hilltop view was awesome. Looking down from the height the monsters looked like pin pricks. He knew he would have to pass them again on the way home but Bobbi knew the fear had gone. That fear hadn't stood a chance when his loving Mum was in control. Mum was happy too. He heard her singing, "Because He lives, I can face tomorrow . . ."

12
Bobbi Gets
a Shock!

Bobbi soon became accustomed to all the laneways around Moorfields. One day he and Mum carefully crossed the busy road onto one of Bobbi Blue's favourite paths. They cantered up the path at a relaxed pace, when SUDDENLY a flock of sheep who had been sleeping behind the hedge rose to their feet with loud bleats of indignation.

Well, Bobbi Blue did what any smart pony would do. He twirled around and bolted for home! Mum had often explained that there

are some healthy fears. But wait! Mum was no longer with him? Bobbi stopped abruptly and turned to see where she was—he found her deposited in a ditch! What was she doing there? He stopped to graze for a minute while he puzzled it all out.

Mum was shouting, "Bobbi, Bobbi, don't go to the road." Bobbi Blue had no intention of going to the road. Mum had spent weeks preparing him for such eventualities. Every time when Mum had dismounted, she had given him carrots out of her pockets. Well Bobbi's training (and greed!) kicked in, and over to Mum he trotted. She rewarded him with copious amounts of treats and told him how wonderful he was. Bobbi didn't know what the fuss was about, but he enjoyed it. It was his turn to tell Mum not to be afraid. Maybe

Bobbi could help others with their fears? Mum got back on and they enjoyed their ride without further incident. Mind you, Mum felt a bit stiffer than usual. She said wryly, "Always be prepared for the "suddenlies" in life. We don't always like them; they are unexpected, but we can be trained and prepared for them."

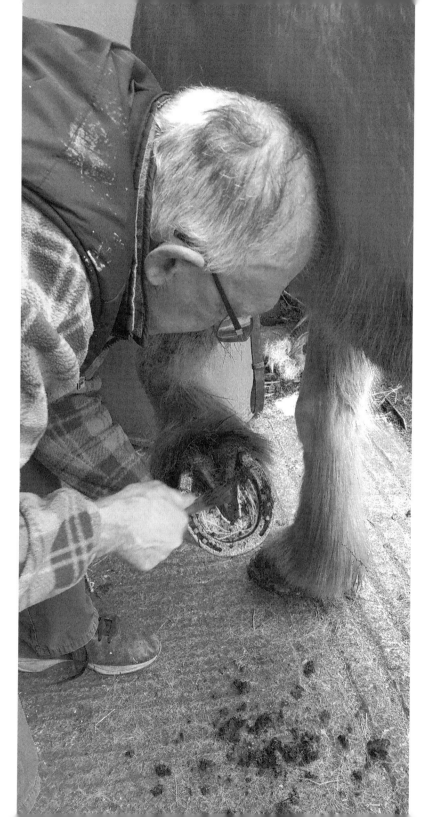

13
Bobbi's New Shoes

Bobbi was just settling nicely into routine when danger struck. He had heard Mum say that a man called Black Smith was coming to visit. Bobbi was looking forward to the visit as all visitors at Moorfields seemed to bring treats.

Black Smith must be very important as Dad had been rehearsing for weeks, picking up Bobbi's feet and shaking hands. However, early one morning Mr. Smith arrived, not bearing treats but carrying instruments of torture including a hammer. He promptly started to cut Bobbi's toes and hammer metal "shoes" on his feet. Mum said these shoes were essential for Bobbi Blue's wellbeing if he wanted to head off on adventures.

Bobbi certainly couldn't comprehend that logic. He wasn't having it! This was terrifying. Life had become very confusing again. What was going to happen next? Bobbi got in such a panic that he reared up on his back legs and accidently hit Dad on the way down. In his turmoil he had hurt the one he loved.

Bobbi was distraught. Then Mr. Smith made a brilliant suggestion. Get Bobbi a bucket of meal! Well, this idea produced a miracle. Bobbi was so focused on his tasty food that he totally forgot about the chaos around him. In no time at all, Black Smith had placed the shiny shoes on all four of Bobbi's feet. This guy wasn't so bad after all and Bobbi strutted round proudly—once the bucket was empty!

Bobbi Blue had learned a valuable lesson. If you want to be shod with peace amid the chaos, be careful what you focus on. Don't dwell on the scary things.

Mum read from the Big Word Book: "Whatever is true, noble, right, pure, lovely, admirable, excellent, praiseworthy—think of these things and the God of peace will be with you."
—Philippians 4:9 NIV

14
The World Around

Bobbi Blue had become very relaxed after several months at his home in Moorfields. He knew that Mum would not allow anything to hurt him, she would protect him from all harm. He had a wonderful love-filled life and everything that a little pony could want. There was always plenty to eat and drink, comfortable places to sleep, fun places to visit. He had his own fan club of family and friends who all loved him even when he was naughty. And Bobbi could be very naughty! He loved his daily schooling, especially now that he had made progress and was learning to jump very high. He often jumped for joy!

Most days Bobbi was very content and happy. But just now and again Bobbi had a bad day. He didn't know why. That made him feel even worse! He was living a life that so many horses would envy, but he just felt fretful at times for no apparent reason. Cattle making strange cries in the distance or his friend Poppy making her loud whinnies made him very anxious. On days like this Bobbi broke out in a sweat and got agitated.

The fear of what was going on in the world around him had crept in unnoticed. It felt like a heavy weight. And it didn't help that Bobbi watched too much television! He is very nosey, so he often pressed his nose against the

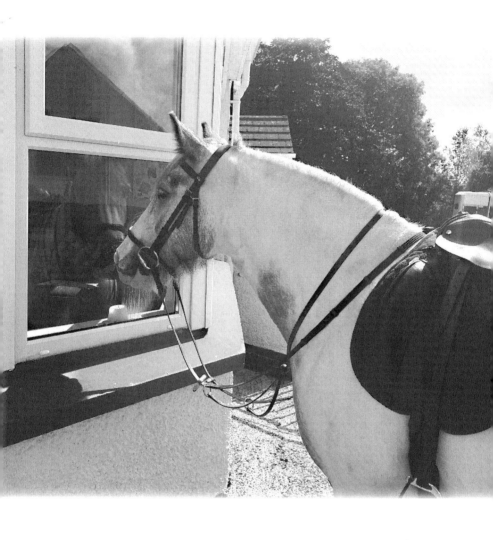

window to see what Dad was looking at on TV or on his tablet. These sights and sounds can be disturbing, and left Bobbi feeling very jumpy, even in his own safe field. When he is having one of these days Bobbi Blue can allow his imagination to think of evil things happening to him and to others, and he becomes unsettled and fretful. That is understandable.

Bobbi needs to be careful what he looks at and what he listens to. But Bobbi Blue doesn't help anyone by being anxious about things that are outside his control. It just upsets him and can even make him feel sick. Bobbi gets a tummy upset when he is anxious. However, Mum lavishes her love on him, promises to protect him and reminds him how kind she has been to him in the past. Bobbi is safe and secure now; most days he experiences a peace that surpasses his understanding. He has learned that he is not responsible for the scary things in the world around him. They are not his business nor his concern; his job is to have fun and enjoy the favour poured out on him. Of course, Bobbi can be kind and helpful when possible but he mustn't fret.

Mum read Psalm 37:1,2 from her Big Word Book. "Do not fret because of those who are evil . . . for like the grass they will soon wither." Bobbi Blue had learned another lesson.

15
Bobbi Blue Gets Dressage Lessons

Bobbi was becoming a very well trained and obedient pony—most days! He had conquered most of his fears and was becoming more confident every day, trusting in Mum's great love for him. However, there is always more to learn.

Mum said she wanted to develop the relationship so that they could ride as one. Bobbi was in full agreement that he had some very bad habits, and so they set off for dressage lessons at a nearby school. The teacher was really nice. She started off with lots of compliments; how handsome and well-behaved Bobbi was (after he had had a couple of naughty bucks!) ...

Suddenly, Bobbi Blue saw himself in the mirror! Oops! (Shock! horror!) It was a scary sight. Did he really look like that? Maybe he wasn't as perfect as he had thought! Mum realised that they were there to learn and was confident that they would make progress. So, after the reassuring praise came a steep learning curve.

The advice began: "Bobbi you need work to be supple. You must go at the same pace until told otherwise. Your transitions need practice." Oh, he had so much to remember and practise! This is how we learn, though, and how our heavenly Father treats us—with love and praise but much needed correction so we can progress, because we are His treasured possession.

Bobbi Blue is on a journey from fear to freedom. Looking back just a few months he has come so far. Love has conquered so many fears as Mum and Bobbi Blue have gotten to know each other. Bobbi knows Mum can be trusted. Life is good and Mum calls Bobbi her perfect pony, even though his perfection isn't quite worked out in reality. That's another story!

From the Big Word Book: "For now, we see only a reflection as in a mirror; then we shall see face to face." —1 Corinthians 13:12 NIV

Shalom

obbi Blue is a changed pony. He knows he is loved and completely trusts his Mum. Horses rarely lie down to sleep in human company. They stand to sleep so they can run away from any fright. Not Bobbi Blue! Now, he lies down at Mum's feet and he even snores! He has experienced shalom—peace, wholeness, completeness, harmony, welfare, prosperity and tranquility.

Bobbi and Mum wish every person who reads this book the blessing of finding this shalom.

"Now may the Lord of peace Himself give you peace at all times and in every way. The Lord be with all of you." —2 Thessalonians 3:16 NIV

DEDICATION

To the those who never gave up on themselves.

CHAPTERS

ACKNOWLEDGMENTS

Thanks is due to those that have supported the cause. I believe that at the peak of success we are only our names. What will your name mean when you are no longer here, who will remember you?

People remember and spread your name – not money, cars, things, etc.

The Accelerated only wants to acknowledge the people.

Sylvester McNutt III

1. WHAT DO YOU DESERVE?

You are going to die.

Not sure when—a genie I am not; however, you will die. One day, you will no longer be able to squander away time and opportunity. One day you will be nothing but dust and ashes. You will be just a memory—or will you? We are beings with expirations. The date that your time runs out remains unknown to all of humankind, which means between your start and expiration, a lot can occur.

I am writing this book because I believe this basic fact has been forgotten. I do not deal with lies, opinions, and fables, which is why I have written a book set in facts and absolutes, one that offers solutions.

You are reading this book because success matters to you; your relationships matter to you; and your finances and your health matter to you. While reading this book you will gain knowledge, perspective, and new skills that will enable you to reach your goals.

When a person becomes aware that he or she wants more, the question that permeates the mind is this: Where do I begin? Success, great health, wealth, financial freedom, physical fitness, and a loving relationship all require the same skills, attributes, and awareness. How do we get to that point? Well, this chapter will tap into one of the most important questions that you probably haven't asked yourself: "What Do I Deserve?" acceleration and becoming accelerated are not possible without knowing the answer to that question.

Acceleration is an analogy for making forward progression, making progress toward one's goal or dream. To be accelerated means that you are clicking on all cylinders, and everything is getting better day by day, such as your health, your business, and your relationship. Acceleration is more akin to a verb; it is the act of doing. Accelerated, on the other hand, is more akin to an adjective. It describes just the way you are.

This book will make someone a millionaire, will assist someone in finding and keeping that special person, and will show people how to obtain and maintain happiness. I guarantee it. This book will show people how to increase the value in their relationships in the business world and with friends and family. The power that is within you is ready to be tapped into, ready to be unleashed. Allow this chapter to captivate your mind, slow down your thought processes, and open your heart as the words herein jump off the page and straight into your veins. There is more than a million dollars of value in this book. Look no further for the secret to love and longevity, to earning a promotion, to losing one hundred pounds, or to taking that big risk. Your first step starts right here.

It all starts here, with this chapter, with you, and with your open-mindedness. To what extent are you willing to allow these words to impact your life? I want you to be a multimillionaire, the person whose relationships improve drastically, and the person who is able to sustain happiness.

For those who read this book and adapt its ideology and tactics, new life, new talent, and new success will be theirs; it works every time.

I want to pose a question to you, the most important question you will ever ask yourself.

First, let everything go, all of your preconceived notions about logic, government, and experience. Just let it go. Allow nothing to exist at this point—no anger, no fear, and no insecurity; just kill it. Your mind should be flowing freely right now; your heart should be open and fears erased. Make room for objectivity and brutal honesty as you answer this question. I am going to ask you three times. If your environment allows for it, read it aloud:

"What do you deserve?"

"What do you deserve?"

"What do you deserve?"

Think about it. Maybe you don't have the answer right now. Maybe the answer is very intricate and complex, and first you have to thoroughly examine your life. Maybe you are already receiving exactly what you deserve. It's possible that you are like most people on this planet and have never considered the ramifications of not having an answer to this question.

If you do have the answer, however, or have consistently thought about this, then you are ahead of the game and are on the fast track to acceleration. Truth is, the majority of people do not ask themselves this, and therefore most people do not have what they deserve in life. Or, from a judgmental standpoint, people's lives will contain elements that they do not deserve. You should be running this question through your head every day—before, during, and after your interactions that add to your total life experience.

This is your wake-up call. You will die, and it will be a lot sooner than you think. Everyone that you know will die, and it will be a lot sooner than you think. Think back just ten or fifteen years, and think about the people who have passed away in that time. People die every day, and they die very often and quickly. They say that life is short, and it's true based on a relative comparison of the average human life expectancy and the existence of this planet on which we operate. Human beings' existence is literally the blink of an eye. So, are you one of those people who walk around thinking we always have tomorrow? If you are, allow *The Accelerated* to stand as your wake-up call.

We have to take our life off cruise control and realize it is our duty to assume control of our life. The time and the experiences that we will or have already encountered are ours, and we own them. The accelerated is a small group, an inclusive, highly sought-after group of people you are about to join. The accelerated just so happens to be a small group of people that realizes one of the greatest secrets to understanding life. They—or should I say *we*—understand that the most important currency that has ever existed is not money. Rather, it is the currency of time. We live, and then we die. We have an unavoidable, guaranteed expiration. We spoil and pass away. This is why becoming accelerated is so vital to living a fulfilled life, a life that will allow you to look back and say, "It was successful; it was blissful; and it was everything I wanted it to be."

Success is yours once you have the answer to the almighty question: What do I deserve? Once you get in the habit of asking yourself what you deserve, you're ready for the next step, which is asking yourself how much time you're using to develop, attract, or create *what you deserve*. Most people really have little to no understanding about the fact that time is an investment, a big choice, and something that should be consistently revisited, as far as how you choose to invest your time. Time never ever goes backward; it only moves forward. Ironically, acceleration is just like time; that is, it continues to move forward. Thus, becoming accelerated will help you align with the course and cycle of life to produce more happiness. Understanding time and what you deserve are choices, success as a whole is a choice. Which choices will you continue to make?

Who defines success?

You and only you define success; you cannot allow other people to set your targets, goals, and achievements. That is simply irresponsible, unless these people can answer the question for you about what you deserve. I believe that only you can answer the question of what you truly deserve; hence, defining success is up to you and only you. Most people will at some point desire the same type of success, such as financial, relationship, fitness, health, parenting, business, and religious/spiritual success. From person to person the parameters will change. One person, for example, might want to bulk up in the weight room, while another person might be looking to reduce his or her weight. Though they have the same goal, they are moving in opposite directions and have a different understanding of what they deserve. Moreover, each person requires a different amount of time to obtain these goals.

Either way, acceleration requires movement and activity. In order to reach a goal, action is required. This is why understanding, embracing, and accelerating forward while being mindful that you define success is crucial to the actual achievement of your goals. Remember, time is not your friend; you will die, and it will be a lot sooner than you think. You define success—no one else. This is the gift of life, and it only comes around once, unless you are some type of human-feline cat animal and you have extended lives? Are you ready to embark on a new journey that will teach, show, and highlight the path to acceleration? You deserve everything you have asked for, everything you have prayed to your god for—you literally deserve it all. The most amazing thing about acceleration is it enables you to get everything you want. There is no shortage of resources when it comes to what you desire. Allow your mind to wrap around that idea again: there is no shortage of resources when it comes to what you desire. A person at full acceleration becomes a person who is accelerated; you move from a verb to an adjective. It moves your life from mediocrity and complacency to rewards, success, and abundance. If you do not know what you deserve, know this: the only thing you deserve is everything you desire. You have the ability to attract, create, and hold all of your dreams in the palm of your hands. If you have ever said, "I wish I was [fill in the blank]," then that is something you deserve and something you are required to create for your happiness. You just have to be ready to accelerate toward your goal—and stay accelerated.

"What do you deserve?"

"What do you deserve?"

"What do you deserve?"

From a high level of understanding you have to ask yourself this question over and over, consistently on a daily basis. There is no reason not to fully understand the scope or to grasp the reality of the answer. To accelerate to a life where you attract everything you deserve, ask yourself this question and create a real answer. It can be a short, straight-to-the-point answer. Odds are, you have a clear picture of what you deserve.

I know that life happens, and I know how hard it can be to really stay positive all the time. Just like you, I have had adversity. I am not above you with my level of adversity, and you are not any less than anyone else because you haven't quite figured it out.

Remember that success and acceleration can occur at any period in a person's life. Success is like a light switch; you have the ability to change your life right now. I know how hard it is when your relationship is not what you desire. I have watched relationships around me fail and falter because of bitterness, arguing, and ego. I have been in relationships that have not worked because I was too immature, lacked appreciation, or did not make my emotion bank available. I have made all the mistakes that young guys make in life when it comes to relationships. I was able to defeat my relationship woes with acceleration and by staying focused on that almighty question: What do I deserve? (What choices will I make?)

Accelerating never stops because what you deserve always changes. Still, you always deserve everything you want. Everyone wants financial freedom, and you deserve it; that's the killer part about it. There is enough money going around on this planet for you to get as much as you desire. You should have a colossal bank account, with access to money well beyond whatever you currently have. Your emergency fund should have multiple zeros in it, and you should be walking around with no debt. If you are not there yet, that's OK. *The Accelerated* will show you the correct behaviors and mind-set to produce income on levels you never imagined. *The Accelerated* has already taken ahold of you and is now pumping more juice, energy, and life into your relationship. You are starting to believe in the answer to that question, and your life is already changing.

Listen, I am the perfect person to help you accelerate; I have taken risk after risk over and over again, all in an effort to create success, health, and wealth for myself and my family. I have moved away from my family, quit my job, traveled with no money in my bank account, slept on floors and couches. I've walked miles to get to a job. I've spent time being homeless, sitting on the curb with a bag of clothes and no direction, asking myself two questions. "What the heck do I do now?" and "What do I deserve?"

I have done it all. I have traveled to multiple states where I did not know a single soul to try and seize an opportunity. When I was in my early twenties, I traveled to Montana to play arena football for three hundred dollars a game and was cut after four weeks. I had no money, no job, and no way to get back home to Chicago, but I made the trip because my dream and my destiny were worth the travel. My dream was worth more than my reality, this is why I stayed relentless and never gave up. I had to ride a bus back home for twenty-eight hours, not knowing what I was riding back home to because I had no job and no place to live. Ironically, I was not discouraged at all; I was motivated by the idea of a new opportunity.

I've been kicked out of school and off a division one football team because I could not execute on my grades. I worked every day for four years to earn that opportunity. I had to bust my ass to earn a spot as a walk-on on the football team. I've been considered an elite athlete with amazing vitals, recovery, and strength for a person of my size due to my understanding of body control, stability, and awareness. However, I did not start that way – when I was born the doctors had to break my legs because of my bow-legged condition and I was stricken to cast for the majority of my first two years on this planet. They told my mother that it would be a miracle if I could walk and play sports.

I've been stricken by a confused ego, lack of confidence, and self-consciousness. I was the guy who had major anger issues and a "f*** the world" attitude. I have had fistfights with both of my brothers, William and Matthew, and have fought my cousin Jason. I was angry in high school as I was suspended for almost fifty days total between my freshman and sophomore year. I fought gang members; I fought in class for no reason. I had an immense amount of anger and hatred for people around me, including my family and friends. I never knew how to control my anger, to speak about my emotions, or let off steam in a healthy way.

I had no outlet for my emotions because I felt like I could only be angry with people. I was just an angry soul who lacked control. I even got fired from Wal-Mart, Jewel-Osco, and one other job. To make matters worse, I went years without speaking to my father because I had petty, unjustified reasons for hating him. I chose to walk around with hatred, resentment, and a lack of respect for my father because I simply did not understand life.

This matters because it all changed when I made a choice; I made a choice based off my answer to the question, the only question that matters, the only question I've asked you over and over, the question you'll read over and over, the question that answers all other questions.

During this same period in my life, I was not able to earn over twenty thousand in a year. I was habitually broke, looking for a family, a girl, or a friend to take me in. I, for sure, had the victim mentality, and my actions showed it. However, Sylvester believed in something greater, I knew that I would make it and be successful I just didn't know how.

"What do you deserve?"

"What do you deserve?"

"What do you deserve?"

Once I was able to answer this question, it all clicked. From there I made a choice. My violent ways needed to disappear. Since then I haven't placed a hand on any person (since I made that choice) I made a choice that education matters, so I have obtained degrees since then. I made a choice that I am not sleeping on anybody's couch, that I would never depend on other people to take care of me. I got my ass in gear, and I accelerated. I did everything I could to attract money. I took real estate classes, acting gigs, and pizza delivery jobs. Sitting still was not an option. In my society and culture, I was never taught about money, so I started reading and acquiring the knowledge that was necessary for me to eventually attract the amount of money that I felt I deserved. I decided that I did not want relationships that were not beneficial, so I did and still do work on myself every day to improve. I want to make sure that I bring some value to the table so my relationship can win.

I was lucky enough to rekindle my relationship with my father. He still loved me and wanted me around, so he welcomed me with open arms. A lot of people do not understand death, but my roommates, a friend, and relatives all passed away. Because I was upfront and personal with death, I understood this idea I mentioned earlier about time. I had to lose control of my fitness level to decide that I would never ever neglect my body again. I went from fit and lean to beer belly at my brother's wedding. I also changed my behaviors and eating habits the next day so that I would stop killing myself. My accelerated action was to start reading books and watching documentaries about juicing and eating organic, with the goal to gain an understanding about food, nutrition, and how my body reacts to certain chemicals. Then, I focused on repeating the action over and over, which produced positive results, I ended up losing over 45 pounds. I also decided that I deserve to write and change people's lives with my talent. Getting a "D" in some poetry class does not mean I should not reach for my dream and my destiny. Although my motivation to write and share with others was derailed, It was simply a roadblock; it meant that I had to try hard, get better, and learn more. It meant that knowing what I deserve every day is the only way I can accelerate toward my dreams.

Today I live a wonderful life. I'm healthy. I live on the West Coast, which was my childhood dream. I played a few years of professional football, another childhood dream. This is my third book, which is yet another childhood dream. I also lead a very powerful sales organization. I have changed many lives with my consulting, advice, and knowledge. I have helped people push themselves toward nirvana, and bliss. I have been able to attract a high level of happiness, success, and knowledge. The best part about it all is I get to look back at the adversity, where I came from, the conversations of people telling me I wouldn't succeed. Those conversations make success so much sweeter.

It is time for you to accelerate and to make that choice, but it starts with that initial question. If you can look at all aspects of your life and say you are 100 percent reaching your potential, then you are accelerated. If not, let's turn off cruise control, let's put our foot on the gas, and let's accelerate toward our goals, dreams, and life that we deserve!

2. LEVELS OF ACCELERATION

The common denominator to all equations of success is time. The variables include mindset, ability and fear. Trust this, the only way your life will equate to success is if you understand your power and understand how to control it. Understanding your power will single handedly cripple or support you in your quest to take your life to the next level.

Acceleration is the *rate* at which the velocity of body changes with time. For example, if a car starts at a standstill and moves forward, the car accelerates. If it decreases its speed, then the car decelerates. It's the same in life. Understand that you are always in a vehicle, and your vehicle is always in motion, just as you, at all times, are accelerating or decelerating in every aspect of your life.

Assigning Meaning

Understanding "meaning" is vital to your success as you focus on creating success. I urge you to be very careful as you describe stories of what these experiences mean, especially as you are going through them. Sometimes, you will have to decelerate because life happens. For instance, you may be expecting to close on a house or business deal, but your child gets really ill requiring not only medical attention but Mommy and Daddy time. The days you spend calling off work or taking time away from your clients is routing you down deceleration from your business goal; however, it is accelerating your duty as a parent. It's vital that we tap into our consciousness and understand the power of our situations. Although one goal is being pushed back, or decelerating, another is being accomplished. I urge you not to get caught up in assigning meaning to every single thing that occurs as good or bad. "Good" and "bad" are relative terms, and they take away from the true understanding of each individual experience. When you judge something as good or bad, you are comparing it to a previous and nonexistent experience.

Assigning meaning to everything will taint your results and your ability to achieve the desired levels of success and achievement you are striving to obtain. Bad things will happen to you that aren't even that bad. Getting a flat tire or someone cutting you off and forcing you to drive an extra five minutes are outside of your control; they are all things you should stop assigning meaning to. What about getting charged an extra five-dollar fee on your account because of some crazy-ass reason that can't be explained to you by a customer service rep who is reading a script off a screen? Such events are unnecessary stress additives that you can not control. They will add stress if you allow them to and, more important, they are stressors that you can let go of right now. If you cannot control it, why assume it is a negative experience? This thought will only generate negative feelings and will produce another negative environment in your life.

Assigning meaning absolutely takes away from one's appreciation of the moment—and the preservation of the current situation. Just because someone says something you do not agree with, do not immediately assign meaning to what he or she is saying because you could be butchering the efficiency of the communication model. Understanding this concept is crucial to developing a life in which you attract what you deserve, creating the success that you desire, and attaining all levels of happiness that you want.

Here's a real-life example to help illustrate the power of assigning meaning. I do not like cigarette smoke or cigarette smokers at all. However, let's pretend I am having a conversation with a girl whom I've just bumped into at the bar. Let's say she is a very attractive woman, and we hit it off right away. What if I see cigarettes in her purse or, even worse, smell it on her? Then I continue in my train of thought— that cigarette smoke is bad. I connect it to my thoughts of, "I don't like cigarettes." Here, I am assigning meaning to my observation, stimulus, or current situation. As a result, two things can go wrong. First, it can break the communication cycle. Second, it can disrupt my appreciation of the now. Now, let's assume I go into a passive-aggressive lane where I continue a monotonous conversation with this lady because I allowed myself to become withdrawn and was unwilling to speak up, yet unwilling to control my own emotional responses to the stimuli.

What if the girl does not smoke, and she was standing outside and the smell just happened to get on her? What if the girl was holding her friend's cigarettes since she did not have a purse that night? I could potentially be talking to the love of my life, just like you could be at any moment. Yet because of what you think you know and your inability to control your emotions, you break the true communication cycle and then lose an opportunity with someone great, simply because you assigned meaning.

With that situation, I hope you see the value in not assigning meaning, allowing the present to thrive, despite what you think you know. Most people struggle with controlling their emotions; most people just act out without thinking about what they are doing. I am challenging you to stop because that behavior does not always allow you to garner the results you desire. You will get into heated debates with your spouse, with your co-workers— even your kids will piss you off from time to time. Only a fool will just lash out and allow the stimuli to control him or her. You control it; you can control your emotions and reactions to events by not assigning meaning. As a human being, you have the innate ability to change and to control almost everything about your behavior. Acting out because of your emotions is a choice; understanding your emotions and, more important, being aware of how they impact your results is crucial for your growth so that you can create the life you deserve. Remember, controlling your emotions does not mean not feeling them. We are emotional creatures, but we are not wild. We have the cognitive ability to be conscious. Most creatures in the jungle respond emotionally because they only know the fight versus flight mechanism, which is triggered by a threat. A human being, who is aware, even in the face of fear, has a choice, a choice to respond in any given fashion. These choices can mean the difference between life and death, which is why it is imperative that, before we start to understand acceleration, creating wealth, sustaining healthy relationships, exuding massive amounts of discipline, or just having fun and being happy as often as possible, we refrain from assigning meaning. Not assigning meaning immediately, understanding the emotions that are triggered, and acting accordingly thereafter with all of the given data will greatly enable you to succeed multiple times over.

Rate and Speed: Types of Acceleration

All methods of acceleration are not created equal. There are different levels of speed on which one can operate. Different goals and objectives require distinctive types of acceleration, although in this section I am going to introduce to you three different speeds or descriptions of acceleration.

A car, for example, has different gears and levels of speed. Poetically, an automobile and the logistics of a motor vehicle really do a great job capturing the essence of acceleration and this model because it is an excellent visualization. When we examine *how* we are reaching, pushing, or creating our goals, we need to value the way we are doing it. Most of the time, knowing the *how* is the missing piece in creating success. Later in this book, I will talk about "execution" and how to execute at a high, consistent level.

Now, back to the illustration of understanding your acceleration path. You will get there in one of three, or maybe even all three, fashions; you will either be a *side street driver,* a *highway driver*, or you will be moving at the *speed of light.* Each will require a different route, mind-set, and physical prowess. Although all three are traveling the same distance, one will use more gas than the other, and one will pump out more exhaust into the universe. There are different risks, problems, and lessons that you will learn on any route you take. Let's take a look at the differences between these avenues and discover why all may be necessary. More important, let's talk about why operating at the speed of light will kick you straight into success, happiness, bliss, longevity, financial freedom, and personal growth.

Side Street Acceleration

I'm from Chicago, Illinois, and one thing I love about my area of the globe is the diversity. Growing up in the Midwest, you learn a lot about adversity, work ethic, and culture. One thing I hate, though, is the design and layout of the city, the traffic, and the overpopulation. I believe that the early settlers of Chicago did not think about the future very well, or at least they did not account for growth. This lack of awareness, planning, and adaptability leads me right to the notion of *side street acceleration*. It is the movement, mind-sets, and actions that operate on a low level of acceleration.

Chicago was the center of expansion and trading for goods and services in the United States; it was known for transportation, as it was the central hub for railroads, automobile routes, and water transportation on the Mississippi River. You would expect that a place with an amazing geographical location would be prepared to accelerate. As a result of white flight, corrupt politics, and an ever-divided citizen group, Chicago has become a volatile, emotionally desolate, and selfish city. The city now has over five hundred murders per year in its majority black populated South- and Westside locations, a city that unites around its sport teams but remains divided by race. This is not a rant against Chicago; however, objectively we must be able to view any situation to understand our "actions" and "results." Side street acceleration produces side street actions; Chicago, then, is a major product of side street action.

I went to college at Northern Illinois University, which is in DeKalb, Illinois. DeKalb is a small corn town about sixty miles west of Chicago. There are about six major expressways that meander through the Chicago metropolitan area in all possible directions. I am referring to DeKalb because of what I learned during my time there. Anyone who is from or who has lived in a small town knows all about the *side streets* and what they enable you to do.

Yes, there is one major expressway that brings an abundance of travelers through the town. It is interstate eighty-eight, but we just call it 88. While I was in college, there was plenty of evil that existed, and much of it abounded on these side streets.

When I use the word "evil," please open your mind because I am not some religious buff who is spewing the word of god or the devil. I'm simply referring to evil as the forces, powers, and activities that exude poison and negativity, the activities that cause you to decelerate—activities we must avoid at all cost.

Those side streets, due to their design and reputation, facilitated drunk driving because people knew the police were too busy patrolling the busy nightclubs and parties at Greek Row. The ergonomics of side streets are dirty, dark, and poorly lit. They are not labeled clearly, and most of them are dead ends, one-ways, or cul-de-sac turnarounds that force you to go back the way you came and try again. Everything in life is analogy; so think about this from a high level of awareness. Empty your mind and visualize a side street. Imagine that a side street is the "path" you have to take to reach your goal, dream, and destiny. Does it sound like the best, most lucrative and most promising path? Does it sound like the type of activity you want to use while you're at the gym or library? Do you think taking shortcuts in the gym or with your finances is going to land you the dream physique or bank account that you deserve? Let's explore some of the other options to understand the different speed, paths, and options available to accelerate toward your dreams.

<u>Highway Driving Acceleration</u>

Highway driving in life is more unpredictable in terms of controlling your success. Some people refer to it as the highway, the expressway, or the freeway. Depending on your location, it is supposed to be the quickest way to get you across the state, from point A to point B. If you live in Chicago, New York, or Los Angeles, then you know the highway is always jacked up full of traffic and other drivers who do not focus on the road. One of my worst experiences was sitting on I-5 in Los Angeles, California. My friend Justin and his wife referred to it as "Carmageddon" because it resembles a post apocalyptic scene out of a movie, where cars do not move or budge at all. I cannot logically process traffic, nor can I understand how people allow it to happen, day after day.

Look, everyone is trying to jump on this mode of highway driving. Everyone wants to get on the highway because they think this is the fastest way—but damn! How can it be the fastest, most efficient way if everyone thinks it's the fastest way? How does that make any sense at all?

Highways produce stress and impatient drivers who constantly practice noncritical thinking behaviors by blowing their horn and jostling for a position to literally go nowhere. If you get off every day at five o'clock and jump on the highway to get home and forty-five minutes have past, I'm wondering if you're still driving home or if you're stuck in traffic. Again, think from a high level of awareness, and let's use this analogy to look at our own behaviors so we can understand if we are highway accelerating ourselves.

Are we getting on the highway (the fast way) just to sit in traffic and create stress? Ever been in a relationship and ask yourself why you were in it? Even if you didn't know why, you still remained in it. Have you ever worked a job where you weren't making any money? Have you hated the managers and the customers you've had to deal with? Have you ever had an apartment, family member, or hobby that just continued to take from you time and time again? Have you had any of these things going on in your life that make you *think* you're moving forward when, in reality, they are slowing you down? Did you stop to look at each situation objectively? I've been guilty of highway driving myself, but I have to remind myself constantly about what I deserve and what it means to have an abundance of success.

If you are sitting on the highway in real life or figuratively, you are wasting your time. We already understand from the last chapter that death is inevitable, and that you are going o die probably a lot sooner than you think. So, what do you deserve? What does your family deserve? What does your relationship mean to you, and why does it deserve to be blissful and accelerated? How much more time will you allow yourself to waste sitting in traffic?

Speed of Light Acceleration

Speed of light acceleration is the holy grail of acceleration. It is the epitome of success. The speed of light is an accumulation of all your experiences, efforts, and desires coming together to push you in one exerted effort to create an energy that is indestructible.

What moves at the speed of light? The speed of light is a universal constant in physics; it is valued at 299,792,458 meters per second. Let's put this into perspective. On the side street, your speed limit is thirty-five miles per hour. If you go over eighty or, in some cases, sixty-five, you will get a ticket for breaking a man-made speeding law that is unjust, while operating your motor vehicle on the highway. If you are moving at the speed of light, in comparison, you are not eligible for any speeding ticket because no officer is capable of moving at that speed. The speed of light is so fluid and moves so quickly that nothing can get in the way. It allows for hiccups and speed bumps, but it treats these instances as minor occurrences instead of major ones.

The reason why so many people have sicknesses, poor relationships, a lack of success, and a life lacking bliss is that they do not operate at the highest level of acceleration, which is the speed of light.

Who operates at the speed of light? How is it that people like Jay-Z, Justin Timberlake, and Justin Bieber have so much success? They all operate at the speed of light. Take, for example, Michael Jordan, Muhammad Ali, and Cal Ripken Jr., all of whom are great athletes whose legacy will live on because of their actions. A solid example of that is how Ali would run in the rain and work out in places all over the country, regardless of racial segregation. The self-proclamation and hypnotism of his own words, "I am the greatest" allowed him to create speed-of-light acceleration. He is legendary; he tricked himself into thinking he was the greatest boxer ever, no matter what obstacle he had to face. Ali had to fight racism, other boxers who were bigger and stronger, and the United States' judicial system. Yet, he persisted and attempted to stay accelerated despite the stimuli. When I say "tricked," believe me; it was a trick. Ali was not born the greatest boxer of all time; it took a constant mind-set of acceleration. He had to create discipline and build confidence and a work ethic that would not falter. He thought about what he deserved and then acted upon it over and over again.

On the night I wrote this chapter, I reached out to my close friend and asked, "Hey, what should I do—watch Netflix or write this next chapter in my book?" Really? What kind of question is that? When we turn on Netflix, we are watching another person live out his or her dream. Every time you turn on that television, you waste thirty minutes of your day watching a show or, even worse, an hour and a half watching a movie. This action—or any action for that matter—that wastes time should be considered deceleration at its highest form. Let's not shy away from the truth I love movies and I own a Netflix account. However, I take careful consideration when watching because I feel like I'm losing part of me to another person's dream. I'm not advising you to stop watching movies, I just want to push your consciousness and aware around what is actually happening.

Of course, I picked up the book and continued writing because I am committed to succeeding and creating a product that will change people's lives. I believe I was born so that I could learn, experience, and then share my knowledge to help others. I am obligated to share my story, my passion, and my worldview because I am certain I can help people.

When you start thinking about the speed of light, your mind starts to transcend to a whole new frame of reference. In his book *Opticks*, Isaac Newton states that it takes the sun's light eight minutes and nineteen seconds to travel to Earth. The speed of light is an instantaneous source of output and force. In 1638, when Galileo tested the speed of light, he set a lantern a mile away from his test subject's eyes. The experiment allowed Galileo to open the lantern and test the duration of time that it took to reach the subject's eyes. The time elapsed was and will forever be instant; he could not find any discrepancy in time.

Think of it as a lightning bolt in the sky—*boom!* The fear of lightning is called astraphobia; this is an abnormal fear of thunder and lightning. You do not need this fear in your life. The fear should be absent in speed-of-light acceleration. In a poetic sense, you are better off *being* the lightning bolt, and with that power it should be your goal to strike everything. You need to strike other clouds; you need to strike people and buildings. Have you ever watched people's reaction to a thunderstorm? They scamper and hide; some light candles while others avoid poles because they think they are going to get struck by lightning. These people do not even know anything about how the discharge of lightning works. They have the same fears about life, in general. You have to eliminate these mind-sets. You do not have the time and cannot afford to be scared of lightning. Be the lightning bolt; strike everything and everybody. You owe it to yourself to make the deepest impact by using the highest type of acceleration possible.

When you operate at the speed of light, when you are in full acceleration, you wake up and, instead of hitting the snooze button, you actually get up. Some even do this with no alarm, some even before the alarm goes off. You move forward with a great workout, breakfast, and when you get in your car for work you have over half a tank of gas. Did I mention your car is actually *clean*? Before you leave the house, not only are your kids ready for school, but the house is clean and the sun is shining. You look into your bank account, and you see the numbers you are looking for. Your relationship is the fairy-tale relationship of which you've always dreamed. Moreover, you are as healthy as can be.

Look, this is not a falsified reality, people. A small percent of us actually live this maximum speed of acceleration. There are many of us who are moving at the speed of light with everything we desire. You, like me, probably have the same goals; I am assuming that you want to be happy, to make your life worth something, and to feel as much love as possible. I am also assuming that you want people around you to be happy. The only way to get happiness is to drive happiness every day with hard work, discipline, and accelerating at the speed of light. The only way to get anything you want is to understand what you deserve— and then go for it.

3. GOALS: MASTER DESTINATION SETTING

It is no secret that goal setting creates a higher level of activity and achievement. This chapter is going to take the bland, basic idea that most people have about goals, and it's going to push the envelope. We can continue to discuss goals as goals, but we'll focus primarily on the accelerated version of setting goals: destination setting. The reason why I want you to think of it as a destination is that now that we are accelerating, we are thinking and acting outside the typical box. It's time to adjust our thinking about certain words and ideas.

Being a middle-class kid, I remember growing up hearing about the richer families taking vacations and going to these amazing destinations, like Hawaii, South America, and the Caribbean Islands. From the poetic standpoint, if you want to get from mainland America to any small island, let's say off the coast of Puerto Rico, what will it require? To get there will require immeasurable amounts of effort and an execution of the plan. Airfare, packing, traveling, sleeping, lodging, dining, and accommodations have to be taken into consideration. To get to the island is possible; people do it all the time.

When I was young, we traveled locally but never took massive trips as a family. To me, it was impossible to get to these places. I had never traveled, and my family never talked about seeing the world, so my view of the world was so small and basic. As a result, I could barely think outside my box to even begin to travel. However, it's not a hard thing to do. One day I had the opportunity to take a road trip to Atlanta, and it spawned my passion for traveling. All it took in order for me to transition from living a life of stillness to activity was to go above and beyond my normal mind-set.

The same analogy goes for extreme goal setting. Think of these massive goals as destinations instead of goals. To reach a destination, we are able to recalculate our plan, exerted effort, and plan of execution. A destination requires an incalculable volume of exertion that should render all other previous efforts insignificant. I'll give you an example of what destination setting (colossal goal) should look like.

Goals are easily obtained in relative terms; a destination comprises a group of goals and is a concept so enormous that it will require you to change your behavior. Destinations can be easy as well, depending on your level of acceleration; however, it should be something that requires you to put forth such an immense amount of movement that you will never register this as easy.

One of my set destination goals right now looks like this: *I am a best-selling author, and I got there by pouring out my unshakeable belief in the idea of acceleration, effort, and attitude. I believe in effort so much that it has been tattooed on my skin for almost ten years. I have changed thousands of lives with this book, which has opened up new career opportunities, nourished relationships, and helped people live a more rewarding life.*

Best-selling author Grant Cardone suggests in *The 10X Rule,* This is the supreme method for setting goals. Muhammad Ali was guilty of this type of self-hypnosis with his "I am the greatest" chant. Kobe Bryant had aspirations as a seventeen-year-old rookie to be better than Michael Jordan and to be known as the best basketball player to ever play the game. Regardless of your personal, subjective view concerning the Michael Jordan/Kobe Bryant debate, the irony is that people never realize it's actually a debate. A legitimate case exists in the argument that Kobe Bryant is the best basketball player to ever play the game. Its achievement was possible only with the belief in self that Kobe consumed and the thousands of actions he took thereafter—*acceleration.*

If you do not enroll in psychology classes in college, chances are, you will never learn about the brain and its functions. I had the honor of going to a Blue Ribbon award-winning school, Palatine High School in the suburbs of Chicago, yet I do not remember any classes that taught us about the power of our brains. I remember social studies, but I don't remember studying vital topics, like understanding emotional responses, processing fear, and thinking about fight versus flight. It's been proven for centuries that setting higher goals drives higher performance. Your ability to set goals as "destinations" instead of regarding them as basic goals will change your performance, attitude, and results.

I often notice in January that there is an influx of activity at the gym, due to all the people whose New Year's resolution is to lose weight. One of the worst things you can do is set a goal because it's trendy or popular. You want to have purpose, reason, and have a belief in your destination (goal setting). Aristotle claimed that purpose can cause action. Once there is a clear destination and purpose, then—and only then—can there be clear action.

Direct goal setting will enhance four major areas: choice, effort, cognition, and persistence.

An entire chapter of this book is dedicated to effort alone, so I'll cover that topic in-depth later on. In that chapter you'll see how effort is measured and applied, and you'll be able to determine whether your life is lacking effort.

Many people underestimate the power of choice. According to William Glasser's choice theory, "total behavior" refers to acting, thinking, feeling, and physiology. Glasser suggested that acting and thinking were the only two that we could directly control. To illustrate how they are intertwined, allow me to ask you a question: Have you ever thought about being sick, hot, or sleepy, and then it actually happened? Truth is, the way you think controls your physiology, or your way of feeling. So, it is imperative that you remain conscious of what you think and how you act. That is why setting dramatic goals will increase your ability to make better choices for your path to success. Those faraway, seemingly unrealistic goals will push you to create more success and land you at nirvana better than weak, immeasurable goals. Push yourself and stop using words like "stretch goals" and "unrealistic"; those words will limit your activity.

Cognition is simply the way you can manipulate and control behaviors that will produce different results; it is the way your thinking processes operate collectively. I spent over a year in a relationship that was useless, unfulfilling, and valueless. Neither of us was intelligent enough at the time to make an attempt to curb our behaviors or set destination goals together. We had no vision, and we were both lazy as hell. I'll never get that year back. What happens if the love of my life dies tomorrow? I am going to wish I had that year back to give to her. Do you see, now, the point? Stop living your life in cruise control.

The definition of insanity is doing the same thing over again the same way—that is, engaging in the same behaviors—and expecting different results. As I was researching for my last book, *Improve Your Dating Situation Now*, I learned that the United States' divorce rate is the highest it has ever been. In one sentence or less, the reason is that *people's behavior does not change*. People think because they can identify a problem in their relationship, they can fix it. I, too, am guilty of this, but the answer is here in this book. To make a change, you must identify the problem, set a new destination (massive goal), and then act in order to see the results. In other words, stop trying to put a square peg into a round hole!

If the goal does not motivate you to make different choices and change the level of your cognition, then nothing will change. If you are able to set the right goal, and then curb your choice parameters and cognition, you can achieve anything.

Remember, when setting a goal, make sure it is a crazy goal that you can measure or track. Make sure that your goal is written down, or that you speak of it as if you have already achieved it. Self-hypnosis is essential in goal setting. And remember, to obtain your goals, a change in thought and in effort are required. Start shifting your cognition now as you shift away from setting goals, and you realize that your biggest dreams are well-thought-out, challenging destinations. I repeat, do not set small, weak, or temporary goals; these will only garner you small success. The goal is to transcend your mind to set colossal, gigantic, and shocking goals because you *can* achieve them. If you really think about it, you already have—so, believe in yourself.

4. THE ACCELERATION MINDSET

The X Factor: Effort and Attitude

I remember being cornered by these two white boys in my school, and being so upset. I felt like they were always trying to pick on and make fun of me because I was black. It's like the thing white kids do to either help you fit in or relate to you. I was young and dumb, and I took it as disrespect. I had so much bottled-up anger that little things like this made me flip my lid. The point is that I did not control my emotional responses to their constant name-calling and disrespect.

I don't back down from any form of competition, so of course I tried to initiate a physical altercation with both boys because I felt like they needed to learn a lesson and respect me as a man. I think I was sixteen or seventeen when this happened. After some huffing and puffing, pushing and shoving, we got separated, and Coach Hayden took us into the shed and slammed the door. Mind you, Coach Hayden was a former football player at Michigan, the only African-American coach/teacher in our school. But he was a badass. He would intellectually whoop anyone's ass in a mental fight. When he'd talk to me, I'd feel dumb, like I knew nothing about life, which I did not; however, he talked with compassion, like he cared and wanted me to learn. His buff shoulders and thick black legs mirrored an NFL linebacker's. In that shed Coach Hayden ripped us a new one: "Go ahead and fight now," he said, yelling, screaming, and getting up in our faces. No one was around, so I'm sure he would have allowed us to fight. And I *was* ready to fight both of them. But none of us budged one bit. In fact, we stood in silence and fear, as there was really only one man there. The three boys who stood in that shed were put back into their place on the totem pole. They *thought* they were men.

Hayden then calmed us down and reinforced the school and team's policy on fighting, which was absolutely forbidden. What you have to understand is, we set a terrible example. I was a black standout football player, and the white guys were ridiculous track stars—and our clashing like that. We were setting the wrong example to our younger team members. We were seniors and we were leaders, yet on this day we forgot about our commitment to lead. We forgot that all eyes were on us. It didn't help being black and having the only black coach in the school demand more out of the black athletes than anyone else. I was ready to quit and go home like a sissy because I felt as if he let them off the hook for their racist comments.

But then my life changed. Coach Hayden looked straight into my eyes, my soul, and sent me a message that would forever change my life: "Sly, the only two things you can control in life are your effort and your attitude."

In cartoons or the movies, you know how the light bulb goes off, followed by someone's spark of genius? Well, that's exactly what happened to me. I kid you not; I was a different person after hearing those words. It literally changed my life and has remained a motivating factor in my daily interactions with people. Hearing those words come from someone I respected, feared, and idolized altered my outlook on life. It was one of the first times I started to grow up and "get it."

I had a rough time in high school. I wanted the world to be a certain way, but it never was that way. I also made a bunch of excuses and did not accept the world as it really was. I was torn between rejection and identity and did not have the proper coping skills to handle tough situations. I wanted people to respect me and see me in a certain light. I wanted other jocks to respect me. I wanted the hot girls to like me and my teachers to respect my intelligence. When a girl did not like me, I assumed something was wrong with her, and when I did not start my senior year initially in football, I assumed the coach was an idiot. I remember feeling like my teachers were too hard on me and expected more out of me than my peers. This mentality is exactly what is wrong with the world we live in. This is *victim thinking*. This is "It's not my fault" thinking. This is *no accountability thinking.* And you or the people around you do this right now; I guarantee it. This is a bullshit way to think about life and will only decelerate you from the nirvana you deserve. Push yourself into thinking that you are the reason for everything—your own failure *or* success. It is up to you, so you must assume responsibility for it. Look, just as I could not control those boys, you cannot control certain aspects of other people. Still, you need to assume responsibility and accountability for your effort and your attitude. These are the only two things you can control all the time, no matter what. So, stop giving away your power to excuses, people, and circumstance. You are not a prisoner of circumstance; rather, you are the creator of your universe.

I remember dating a girl who was extremely promiscuous. Even while we were dating, she used to get around like a bad cold. I used to think that I did not give her the sexual pleasure that she needed. Although I was, I felt like it was my fault. She cheated on me, I thought, because I did not give her the communication and trust she needed. I remember trying to take her phone from her, or to make her see my value. I remember trying to argue with her about what I could do for her. The point to my story is this: I learned from that situation and tried to improve on these behaviors in my next relationship. My effort and attitude were and are the only things I can control. I was a damned fool to think that I could control another person, especially a woman. There is no person strong enough on this planet to control another person. People can barely control themselves. Once you understand that, you'll be able to focus on you.

Truth is, you do not have the power to control another person. Think about how many so-called god-fearing, god-following people commit sins such as molesting children, raping innocent women, or taking the lives of people who have posed them no threat or harm. Look, if your god cannot control another person, what makes you think you can? You cannot control another person, and thinking that you have the ability to do so will only set you up for failure. But you can, at all times, control your effort and your attitude. You can, at all times, hold yourself accountable for your actions, your efforts, and your results. Forward movement is required. You will accelerate toward ultimate success when you embrace the knowledge that you can control only your effort and your attitude. Remind yourself. Text yourself, circle it in this book, or highlight it so you can remember it: the only two things you can control in your life are your effort and your attitude.

The Motivating Factor: Knowing Your *Why*

The only issue with striving for success or greatness is the measurement of it. What is the difference between something and someone who is amazing? The most important part of anything you do is knowing *why* you do it. The *why* will stand as the forever growing motivating factor in why you operate the way you do.

Never get caught up in the *what* (activity) or the *how* (execution). Focus instead on the *why* (motivating factor). *Why* is the most powerful, inspiring reason for motivation that exists on this planet! For example, if you were to tell your significant other, "I'm with you because I like you." Sure, that may be true, but it is only telling him or her *what* you are doing. You may tell this person that you are going to send him or her a love letter, comfort that person, and make that person feel special; however, this is only telling that person *how* you are going to love him or her. To truly understand the power of love and success, you have to understand and express the *why*. Here is an example of a statement that entails the *why*: "I am with you because

38

you make me feel like no other person can. I believe in you and want to accelerate my life with you. I am dating you because of all the seven billion people on the planet, you are the reason I wake up every day. I cannot live another day of my life without you. When we combine we are a complete whole."

You have to transition from the *how* and *what* to the *why*. Once you can fully identify the motivating factor for your actions, you will be able to build the bliss and nirvana that you deserve. Simon Sinek presents this idea of the *what, how, and why* as the golden circle. He says it is entangled in our biology, not our psychology. Sinek says that companies who market to the *why* part of the brain create more sales than others, citing Apple as a reference.

Knowing the *why* is and will always remain the motivational factor you will need to achieve greatness. I want to share with you my *why*. As we accelerate together, it is important that you understand what motivates me. I would love to know what motivates you as well.

Sylvester's *why* is leadership, sacrifice, and motivation. I was put on this plan to lead people. I believe that my life has been adverse and full of pain to gain perspective and experience so that I could become a more powerful leader and motivate people. I have been kicked out of my house, kicked out of school, and kicked out of people's hearts over and over. I have failed over and over again. I've had business ideas crumple underneath me. I have watched my bank accounts grow and fizzle to nothing. I believe with all of my heart that I have been mentally abused, discounted, and left for dead. I am 100 percent positive that my life has been created not for me, but for other people. I am so confident in this that I believe I am the sacrificial lamb for my goal. My goal is to inspire, motivate, and help people curb their behaviors to turn their lives into bliss and success.

I have been a selfish, egotistical and, at times, lazy person. I have been a self-entitled, arrogant sissy at times. I, too, just like most people, have struggled with my identity, my appearance, and my motivation to move forward. The reason that I am able to get up every morning is that I know my way; I am here to be an agent of success. I am here to give people hope and insight into another way of life. I desperately want to impact people's lives forever, but I will have only a few short breaths and then I will be gone. I believe that you cannot hate on a person who wants to give love and motivation. When people think of Sylvester McNutt III, regardless of their personal vendetta or opinion, I want them to say, "That guy is a hard worker, and he has shown me that I can do anything I set my mind to." I believe in the power of thought and the laws of attraction. I believe that the mind is the greatest and most powerful tool that exists. I will tell my kids this from birth: you can do everything you set your mind to do. I have seen people lose weight, change minds, create all types of revenue with nothing but an idea. I believe that if I stay in the lane of acceleration, I will attract people like you, and you will attract other people, and so forth. I believe that we will build an army together that will change the world. I am not a million people, but I believe that my thoughts can get to a million people in a day and can inspire the next world leader, the next agent of success, or the next person who will create some type of nirvana for all of us. My last book on relationships was written because I wanted to improve people's relationships, but I realized that I needed to go back and create this book, a book on improvement, success, and personal growth. We have to push ourselves toward our potential, and in order to get the best out of others, we have to operate on our highest levels. Look, I love children and relationships, and children deserve to have loving relationships. I believe the most important thing we do is create and build relationships. It is vastly valuable to me that we understand ourselves, create a lane of acceleration and, last, but most important, we never ever forget the reason *why* we do what we do. What is your *why*?

Master the Situation: Know Your Product. Know Your Customer.

This may sound like a chapter about sales, and that is because it is. Owning my own business, being a sales manager, and being a dominating salesperson has taught me the key to success in sales, relationships, and life. It is the most important thing a person needs to know about improving life and trying to build, create, or drive something such as revenue or love.

You have to know your product and your customer. Think big, think massively, so that this analogy resonates with you and impacts your life today.

Who are your customers? More important, who are their salespeople? You are a salesperson, and every person you interact with is a customer. Every person you touch, talk to, or see is a customer. Your customers are buying you, your time, your conversation, and your ideas. Customers are your children, your lovers, your classmates, your teammates, your employees; and you yourself are indeed your own customer. Think on a high level of awareness here. Think like a fly on the wall watching you day to day. You are selling ideas, metaphors, and a lifestyle every day. The simplest task, like telling your children to pray, or to wash their hands after they eat, is an idea—an idea that you are selling.

Stay with me here. I need you at your highest level right now. Understand that you are your product—at all times. A client of mine sells personal training for a living. One of the obstacles he had to overcome was the fact that he did not see himself as a salesperson. He saw himself only as a trainer. I prodded and planted the seed that he is *not* a trainer; he is actually a sales trainer, and then his business transformed. He doubled his profits after his realization. Remember, you are selling yourself at all times.

Even when you start to apply this knowledge to other areas of your life, you see that knowing your product and customer are the most important.

Here is the perfect example of the product-to-customer relationship. Regardless of your dating situation, think back to a time when you were single and looking for the perfect person. If you are single, then this is the perfect activity to understand the product-to-customer relationship.

Imagine the most beautiful, loving person you will ever meet stepping into your life today. But it comes with a question, and the question is this: Why should I date you? You could go on with fifty different reasons that will have little to no effect at all. The way you utilize what you know about yourself (product) and what you know about your customer (your potential loved one) is what will get you the girl or guy of your dreams.

Think back to the last chapter on knowing the *why* (motivating factor). Take that same situation and then link the *why* to your conversations and, more important, to your actions, and your result will be different. If the person asks you why he or she should date you, you may be a poet with words, but you'll finally have the perfect answer. You have to know what your customers desire in order to get them in your lane of acceleration. You have to understand what your customers deserve; you may be the right person for them simply because they deserve a person like you.

Look, when I promoted clubs in downtown Chicago, there was nothing on paper that separated me from any other promoter. Yet, when I had conversations with people, I realized I booked more parties than I could keep up with. I was booking so many parties that I had to get another cell phone, create another Facebook account, and get my best friend to join the scene with me because I could not handle the business alone anymore.

What did I know about my customers? Hell, I knew they were in their early twenties, fresh out of college, but thirsty to be on the scene. I used that to my advantage because most kids out of college are broke. I pitched it to them as if I were some celebrity, but I was taking the time

43

to get them out of their comfort zone and out to clubs that had three and four thousand people in them. I would tell people, "Sure you can go to another club, but I am going to make sure you have the best experience with me; do not worry about anything." I assumed all responsibility for their nights. Keep in mind the parties I booked were in the twenties and thirties. One night, I remember I had a party of seventy and two separate parties of fifty people, all at one time. I had so many people trying to get in the club at one time that the bouncer shut down the whole operation and told me that I brought too many people. Some of you may look at it like, how is that a good thing? Success is success when your old problems go away and you have a new set of problems. My problem before was that I was broke, and then I started doing this business. My problem then was the demand was too high, and I couldn't do it alone—new problems. Why is it that I was able to drive so many people to one location to party instead of another? It's because I knew what they wanted down to a tee. I listened and asked open-ended questions, and every time this happened I connected my physical product and me as a single product in every transaction. I connected my personal commitment to ensuring that they had the best experience possible. Other promoters were more connected than I was, had a better ride, and had way more money. I did not even have a car when I was promoting. The only thing I had was skill, work ethic, and determination.

I am giving you my secret right now; connect your product to your customer. It will work every time. When it does not work, assume your effort was displaced. From a business standpoint, I will tell you the exact strategy that I used. It may help you tremendously.

One day, when I was looking at the ergonomics of Facebook, I noticed they had a calendar where you could see everyone's birthday. I got really creative and opened up a blank Microsoft Word page and started typing away. I made a template of a handcrafted message that I would send to people who had a birthday coming up in the next ninety days. The template was something I just made up. I asked myself, "What do people deserve for their birthday?" I then tailored the message to each person and sent it out to every person on my page when he or she had a birthday coming up. From there, I would hop on the train and go to downtown Chicago. I was hungry and thirsty, literally. I wanted to make a change in my life, and I was able to see that my vision was not my situation. Carless, jobless, and staying in my grandmother's basement after being cut from an arena football team was my situation; but my vision couldn't be more different. I knew my product, which was Sylvester, and I knew that I could see the end result of greatness.

When I was in downtown Chicago, I would walk around and talk to random people and try to get them to come to this club. I got paid per my head count. I spent all afternoon walking around and selling stuff, regardless of how bad my feet hurt, regardless of how much people told me it was not worth it. Then I remember walking in the club and Mike Doujai, the guy who got me into the promoter game, handed me $500 in cash for my efforts. Five hundred may not seem like a lot of money to some people, but, again, this became a repeated behavior and result for me. Since I knew my product and my customer, I was able to change my life with my actions.

From a different perspective, let's look at Apple. How is Apple so successful? How is it that they are able to win in the game of technology while others fail? I am going to tell you why. They were smart enough to use the word intuitive. Most people are terrified of change and are therefore terrified of change in technology. The average person cannot tell you anything about technology. People own and allow their technology to dictate their lives, yet they know nothing about their refrigerator, their car, or their cell phone. Hell, how many people actually know how electricity is created and conducted? Seventy percent of people will not change if they do not have to, as change is one of the scariest things that can happen. This emotion and feeling is what Apple captured. They used the fear of change and technology to captivate millions of people by calling their products easy to use and intuitive. As a result, people have changed their perspective; technology is no longer terrifying. People buy these products because they know they are easy to use. Connect the product to the customer. Truthfully, their products are not "easier" to use; in fact, I've watched thousands of people struggle with using these Apple devices. If you don't believe me, go stand in Best Buy for an hour and listen to some of the questions customers ask.

Let's take this idea and apply it to a dating situation. The love of your life will become and remain the love of your life only if the product (you) is consistently connected to the customer's (spouse) desires and wants. Again, you define success, and only you. It is irresponsible for anyone else to set goals for you. If your goal is to make your relationship a fulfilling one, then know your customer and product. Think high level again; open your awareness and realize that you are in sales. Your life is about sales and selling ideas; moreover, it is about selling your truths and your thoughts. I need you to become an expert on yourself, your kids, your job, your parents, your children, your car, and your god. I need you to become a master of your fate.

To master anything—or to sell anything or to obtain any level of success where you must convince, persuade, or demonstrate the value of a product—remember that you have to know inside and out your product and your customers' wants. You have the advantage. You know the answer to the question, *What do you deserve?* Turn the table and think about what *they* deserve. Once you can answer that, you will accelerate to the highest level.

The Wealthiest Mind

It makes no difference what your goal is in the physical and tangible sense because one thing remains constant. If your mind is not rich, if you do not feel as if you deserve success and are willing to maintain it, then you never will. If I handed you one million dollars today, would that make you a millionaire? No, you physically would be holding a million dollars, but you would not be a millionaire. The presence of a million dollars is nothing but a possession, the holding of paper. Holding a million dollars will never make you a millionaire, nor will it make you a happy person, solely based on the possession of it.

Being broke can make you unhappy as well. Nirvana and true

bliss is maintained when you feel rich consistently but not just rich in terms of your access to finances. I am referring to rich in the sense of your personal total fulfillment. No matter your situation currently, if you do not have the mind-set of wealth for every avenue in your life, you will be broke.

Your relationship will be broke; the relationship with your parents will be broke; your job will be unfulfilling; and your financial situation will always remain turbulent—until you make a choice. Why do people who are extremely wealthy from a financial standpoint appear to be happy? My friend asked me, "How do you walk around with a smile all the time and have so much motivation? You have a great life and a better situation than most people, so why don't you just slow down?" This type of thinking is part of the problem. This is why it is so important that you are conscious of what you think and what other people think about around you. To whom is she comparing me when she asks me that question? Just because I have access to a certain amount of money, does that solely make me happy? She has a poverty consciousness; she has a minimal way of thinking. She does not set destinations; she is only setting self-defeating landmarks of failure. I am happy most of the time because my mind is wealthy; I already feel rich every day because I do not think that way. You have to create a feeling of wealth; you have to repeat affirmations of wealth. The mind is the most sensitive tool on this planet; you have to be very conscious of what you think. When you allow yourself to think negatively, too small or too narrow, you will notice that your results will be a direct reflection of them. Your mind will have a sensory reach of whatever you desire;

call it self-hypnosis if you will.

Remember when I told you earlier that Muhammad Ali used to say that he was the greatest? Ali was not born the greatest; he became the greatest through his consciousness and his actions working in unison over multiple hours to perfect his craft. Nobody is born a genius, rich, or extremely healthy; these are all choices that a person can make.

Here is a real-world example: Why do basketball players practice on the court they play games on? Why do track coaches tell their athletes to sprint, throw, or jump at their maximum ability before their actual event? Why do you think a guy or girl gets a bunch of attention from the opposite sex? These things are visualized and practiced; they are sensory rich and self-hypnotic with repetition. I could take the guy with the lowest self-esteem on the planet and tell him he is going to do twenty minutes of abs a day; he will write down five positive things about his behavior daily, and he will then attempt to smile at people more every day. I am over 100 percent sure that he would widen the gap from the fear of mediocrity and low self-esteem; yet, he would position himself into a lane of attracting an amazing new life. He would become the sexiest guy on the planet; he would attract a wealthy lifestyle and a life of acceleration. I would make this guy push his normal boundaries and challenge his status quo. I would demand that this guy stop using words like "low self-esteem," and I would introduce him to new words that push his consciousness to a whole new level.

Money is easy to make. Just walk into Wal-Mart and Target, and you will see people who walk around aimlessly with no destination, picking up random merchandise that they do not need, looking to spend their money on things that look cool. Have you ever walked into the store looking to buy a five-dollar item, but by the time you check out you are buying eighty dollars' worth of stuff? This happens all the time, all over the world.

I have sold items to people just by knowing the customer and knowing the product; I have sold my time, services, and ideas just by believing in them and showing their value. You are no different; you can make colossal amounts of money starting right now by pushing your normal thoughts and transforming them to abysses of success. Stop thinking you are broke. Stop thinking there is something wrong with money. Ideologies that block your total output should be tamed, or irrelevant, moving forward. You deserve bliss, happiness, and all the success you want, but you have to push the envelope. You have to take risks and chances, even when you do not know the outcome. It's a matter of seeing the last step, taking the first one, and not knowing anything that is going to happen in between.

Since I was put out of the house at the age of seventeen, I have been determined to never depend on my parents for help. I love them, but I made a decision to never ask them for anything. I have been so focused on creating my dreams that I spent the last $300 I had on a plane ticket to fly from Chicago to Billings, Montana, just for an opportunity to play professional football. I was there for a few weeks, didn't get any playing time, and spent the money I had while I was there, but I busted my ass every day. I worked hard to make the idea come to life. Because of some behind-the-scenes politics, I was cut and left homeless with no income again. Then perseverance kicks in, and you just move on to the next thing. You can harvest anger and be pissed off, but if you do not transfer the energy into good, then you are slowly killing yourself. Attracting money is easy; you just have to think about it and believe that you deserve it.

Your relationship is no different from your money. Wealth is not just about accumulating a colossal amount of money. Being wealthy is about having the total package at abundant levels. What benefit is it to have access to twenty or thirty million dollars right now as spending cash when you cannot walk up the stairs? What good is it if your phonebook is filled with names or people who don't even know you, and you are just a lone soul who is secretly dying inside? Pick up the phone, find out which six people will carry your casket, and call them now. If you do not have these people already, go out to events and find people. It is a fact that you need human interaction to be happy.

The mind is the most powerful tool to create wealth, health, and forever-lasting nirvana. You cannot and will not achieve it if you do not become aware of your subconscious. The power is in thought; the power of everything that exists is in the thoughts you have.

Here is one clue that is ridiculously valuable, so important and crucial to your life. Anything you believe in, think about, or give power to will exist and manifest in your life. Everything will come from what you believe and what you act upon. How else would you explain amazing human feats such as flying? Like Olympic sprinters running over a hundred meters in fewer than ten seconds or people in our generation like Mark Zuckerberg, the creator of Facebook, captivating the planet with an idea. How is it that Michael Jordan, a man who got cut from his high school basketball team, was able to grow to be the most celebrated athlete of all time?   What about inventions that have changed the world as we know it? These are all just beliefs and thoughts put into action. Look at Joseph Woodland with the barcode or the mobile telephone created by Bell laboratories in 1946. Or, what about British computer scientist Sir Timothy John Berners-Lee? You may not know who he is, but his idea will live forever. He is the inventor of the World Wide Web.

Every goal is a belief and an action away. Take as many risk and chances as you can. You never know when something will be a hit, make you rich, or create that feeling of joy that you deserve. Always stay focused on your destinations and what you allow into your consciousness. This is how you grow, develop, and train yourself to have the wealthiest mind.

5. STEER IN THE LANE OF PERSEVERANCE.

"Do you know the definition of perseverance, Miss Melas? Continuing in a course of action without regard to discouragement, opposition, or previous failure," said Alex Hitchens, a character played by Will Smith in his hit movie *Hitch*.

Success is not easy, and to be fair, you probably will not find yourself anywhere near it if you do not persevere. A lot of people make it look easy, but trust me; there is a lot of failure, struggle, and pushback that occurs when you strive to reach your destinations. However, it is so important that while accelerating you do it at the speed of light and stay in the lane of perseverance.

With this line, Hitch was telling his future wife that although you have no interest in me right now, I am going to try so hard to be with you that you and I will both see that there is no other option. He was psyching himself up and remembering what he deserved; he was letting her know that no matter how much conflict she brought, no matter how hard it got, no obstacle would be strong enough to stop his will.

This is the level of perseverance we must strive for in the quest of our dreams. Look at former Olympian and motivational speaker, Derek Redmond. The video imagery he's featured in embodies perseverance. In the 1992 Olympic Games in Barcelona, Derek tore his hamstring in the middle of the four-hundred-meter semifinal. Tearing your hamstring is one of the most petrifying and excruciating injuries that could happen. I'm familiar with the suffering, agony, and terror it causes when a person rips such a dynamic muscle. Upon tearing his hamstring, Derek did not give up. He persevered through the pain and the fact that the race was lost. There was no way he was going to come back and win against other Olympians who were healthy and still moving forward as he remained knelt to the track. With about half the race left, Derek trotted, skipped, and hopped his way to the end of the race. Tears streamed down his face as the pain of finishing was too much to bear. Yet, he did not give up. His father ran out from the crowd to accompany him; regardless, he would not stop. The scene was so poetic as his father pushed through security yelling, "That's my son." On one good leg, with tears streaming, and with his father on his arm, Derek finished the race. The time did not matter; his last-place finish did not matter. The man was determined to finish the race. Although he trained and strived to be Great Britain's gold medalist, looking back, we are able to see that the only person who knows who won the gold medal that year was the person who actually won the gold medal.

This is what we have to understand: sometimes, it's not about the place you finish in. Sometimes it's just about standing up with whatever you have left and saying to yourself, "I am going to get this done no matter what happens to me." You are the most powerful deserving being in the universe, and it starts and ends with your ability to persevere. Trust me, we all know how hard it is when things don't go the way you expect. However, you have to stay focused on your goal, your dreams, and what you deserve. This clip can be found on various video sharing sites, but it will go down as the model of what it means to persevere through the conflict. If you have not seen this clip, I urge you to watch it right now, and then come back to read this book.

For the accelerated, the application of perseverance is required. You have to accept that things will not go the way you planned. Life will be a lot harder than you anticipated, and at times everything is stacked against you. There is nothing fair about this world, the people, or systems we have created. This does not give you the excuses to settle, lie down, and be worthless. You deserve a life of bliss and happiness in all aspects. You deserve to accelerate at the speed of light. Staying committed to the process of perseverance is the only way you will reach, achieve, or become anything.

One of my customers is bound by a wheelchair, has poor vision, cannot use his legs, and is utterly lonely, but he never complains to me. If people do not attempt to open the door for him, he will try his best to do it for himself. The man comes by my office from time to time just to say hello. He says to me, "Hey, do you mind if I stay awhile? You're playing some good music." Then he just lies back in his wheelchair and listens to soul R&B. He does not allow his circumstance to disrupt his attempt at bliss. He is more accelerated than adults who are willing and able to make a change in their own lives but refuse to because they accept lazy, complacent, and downright disrespectful results.

One final point about perseverance: life will not give you anything. Stop playing the lottery with your life. You deserve to have more control than a random pull of the numbers. This is not a game; this is your life. It is your responsibility to do everything in your power to create an amazing life, a life where everything is operating at its full potential. You deserve a life in which your child has more love than he or she knows what to do with. You deserve a life that has an abundance of opportunity and financial security. There is no reason why your bank account shouldn't be oozing over with zeros and commas. There is no reason why your children shouldn't be your best friends and talk to you about everything. It makes no difference if you are a business owner or an employee. You should be the best at what you do. Remember, you deserve bliss, and you deserve to operate at the speed of light. You deserve to be in the top 1 percent of the people who reach all things they desire. What do you deserve?

6. STOP GETTING DRUNK AND HIGH

Expand your consciousness and think high level; I need you to believe that this chapter is not about alcohol and marijuana. I need you to believe that this chapter is bigger than drugs and poison in only the physical format. The route I am trying to take you on is the one less traveled. What do alcohol and marijuana have in common? They both alter, impair, or manipulate your normal train of thought. Again, you have to read this objectively because I am not saying that either is bad or good; this is your choice to make. I am saying that you have to be conscious of what enters your bloodstream; I am saying that both of these upon entering your bloodstream alter your normal state of awareness. Remember, your thoughts and your consciousness become your actions. This is why it is imperative that we access what we are allowing into the stream.

Would you let someone inject you with an IV that was filled with chlorine? No, you would not. Why not? Well, you do not want to die, be poisoned, or put things in your body that are not good for you. You are fully aware of the damage that chlorine may cause because the warning labels tell you that after consumption death is possible.

I need your highest level of consciousness right now because what I'm about to drop on you is monumental. There are people in your life, hobbies in your life, and other things in your life that are poisonous. There are people whom you allow to enter your bloodstream. These people do nothing but kill you; they warp your mind and body, and, ultimately, they decelerate you from your dreams. I guarantee that if you, right now, picked up your cell phone and scrolled through your contacts, you'd find at least one person you do not like because he or she is negative, poisonous, or vile. YOU might even be this person now. That's right; you might be the person who is killing yourself (remember our discussion about the power of assuming all responsibility).

When I was single and partying, I used to live "the life." Go ask anyone who used to hang out with me. I was between eighteen and twenty-five years of age. My parties were the best parties. We used to either throw the party or get into the party for free, and there were always attractive women around. Hell, I am a good-looking guy with a lot of confidence and connections, so why would women not want to hang out with me? There was a guy I'd occasionally let into my circle, but he would come around only when there was a guaranteed chance at hooking up with a girl or at least having a conversation with an attractive woman. Yet, the parties and the people at them were my parties and my connections, so he was benefiting and winning off my strength. But it became a problem when we were cleaning up the mess, taking cab rides back to find our cars, and trying to pick up the pieces from a destructive night. This person was nowhere to be found. (I'm not condoning the dysfunctional behavior; I'm simply recalling a story and sharing it with you so we can learn from it.) The point is that this dude would only hang out with me when he knew he could benefit, and if there was no benefit, there was no communication, connection, or conversation. I was young and naïve and assumed all these guys wanted to be my friend, but I was wrong. This guy went so far as to try to hook up with every girl I talked to or had my eye on. Really, dude? Mind you, I threw parties in college; I worked at the bars in college, and after college I spent time promoting the hottest nightclubs in Chicago. I was the guy you needed to know—not to mention the market for black promoters was not that strong. It's easy to say that I was known for this. Some people knew nothing about my playing football in college. Another valuable lesson we can learn from this guy is this: when you build a dream and network, like the one I built, it is your duty not to allow freeloaders in your environment. Freeloaders are poisonous creatures. Plus, nobody should be allowed to ride for free, especially if they are poisonous. I'll give you some more examples of people who are poisonous:

- The relative who asks for money every time you see him or her
- The ex who only calls to hook up
- The other parent of your child who tries to pit your child against you
- The lazy boss who tells you that you do not work hard

- The person who asks you to do things against your morality
- The friend who does not respect your relationship with your significant other

These people can decelerate you. Remember that you cannot control them and that success creation is solely up to you and your actions. Controlling only your effort and attitude, and not theirs, will create the bliss that you are accelerating toward. To create success you have to monitor the poison that you allow into your life; you have to monitor the freeloaders and stop allowing people to leech off your energy. In the game of life, when we are moving forward, we should be willing to avoid all dysfunctional behaviors. If you are in a dysfunctional relationship with someone who is silently killing you, my question to you is this: How long can you survive?

7. YOUR ROSTER AND COMPETITION

In the last chapter, I talked about avoiding poisonous people, preventing freeloaders from using your energy, and focusing on not allowing dysfunction to operate in your relationships. With that being said, we need to access your team. Whether you realize it or not, you have a roster. In any team sport, there is a roster of people who are going to help create results.

For the sake of ease, let's use a basketball team that consists of five starting players, eight or nine bench players, a head coach, and a few assistant coaches. Let's take it a step further. We also have strength and conditioning coaches, athletic trainers, and equipment personnel.

All have different roles, responsibilities, and attributes that they bring to the table, yet every person's contribution is valuable.

Any person who has been a part of a team sport understands that it does not take the effort of one to win. We also understand that it does not take only one effort to lose. It takes a grave amount of effort just to show up to the party and make a difference.

The reason that I want you to wrap your mind around the idea of thinking about the people in your life as if they were on a roster is this: if you don't look at the team, you will never realize the dream. I urge you to be humble enough to realize that you probably will not achieve what you want without the help of others. When I look back on times when I was homeless or my cell phone got shut off, I realize there were people who stepped up and allowed me to sleep on their floor or their couch. Some even paid the bill for me to get my phone back on. I am self-made, yes, but only with the help of others. You have to know who is on your team, and you have to understand that day in and day out. If you look at the Michael Jordan Bulls, or any of the championship Lakers or Celtic teams, you will see a commonality that is so basic, it is often overlooked: the commonality that NONE of those teams was the same every year. There were tweaks, changes, and major developments that caused all of those teams to change, such as roster changes, scheduling, and personal ability.

Even those who wash the practice jerseys, plan team meals, or control what plays are being called can drastically change results.

This book is about success and creating wealth, health, and true bliss. The only way we are going to do that is with effort, a plan, and a laser-like execution of that plan. This is why it is imperative we examine who is on our roster and determine their value. For example, is this a person we can develop? Is this a person who has the championship attitude? Is this a person who needs to be cut?

Now, one might say professional basketball is a business, and I am going to tell you that you are right, and you are a business, too. You are no different from a company such as Apple or IBM. If you do not put the right people in the right place, balance your assets, and create success for yourself, then the other teams will dominate you, or, in this case, you will get dominated by other people. This is important, and it needs to be important to you.

When my daughter asks me to feed her, she does not give a damn about how tired I am, how I allowed the wrong people on my roster, or how I made excuses my whole life. When my son asks me for money to take a girl out on his first date, and to borrow the car, how do you think I would feel if I told him that he cannot go because I did not bust my ass enough when I was his age? How would he respond when I tell him that I allowed poisonous people in my network and on my team?—and now we have no money, no access to anything, and, worst of all, we don't have the will, drive, and determination to create anything. My kids will not accept those answers, and you shouldn't either. It's time to reassess the people in your life. Ask yourself why they are there. You may already know the answer. I am not telling you to do away with everyone and just start over, but then again, maybe that is what you need to do.

I have moved across the country many times to chase my dreams and to create an opportunity for my family and myself. We are not rooted anywhere; rather, we are people who have the mobility to go anywhere we want. We are not rooted to people, either, so do not fool yourself into thinking that you are required to be friends with someone simply because you guys have been friends for a few years. The people in your life are assets, so it is very important that you take the command to add value to their life and vice versa. If you are just a taker and demand people's time, money, and energy, but you do not add any value to their life, then you need a wake-up call. Similarly, if someone is just leeching off you, you need to kick him or her in the ass and demand that he or she makes a change. Remember that you can control only your effort and your attitude; it is up to you to determine what action you take to do that.

The people who really know me know that I believe in hard work and building relationships with people who will work hard alongside me. If you do not bust your ass every day, you might as well jump ship because I am steering it down the lane of perseverance and acceleration. My people know that I have an undying will to create success and nirvana in my life. I wish you could hear my phone conversations with people; I am constantly trying to add value to our conversation by pushing people and challenging them. So what if they don't like it? If they improve, then I have achieved my goal of trying to help other people.

Some wise guy is going to say, "Well, what if I don't need to be challenged or pushed?" I will offer you my opinion. First of all, shut up. Second, that's nonsense. Everyone needs to be pushed, even me. Some people push me hard, really hard, and they push me past my potential. That does not demotivate me. Everyone needs a challenge and a destination that is set so high that it seems unachievable. Everyone needs a network, and everyone needs to monitor who is on their active roster at all times. Remember that everyone has a role and will contribute to your success, and you are required to add value to people's lives as well. If any of this sounds crazy or unrealistic, then I dare you to underperform in your marriage or at your job. Your spouse, employer, and customers will be dropping your ass like a bad habit. The accelerated find ways to build, grow, and maintain networks that produce for them, and it starts by weeding out the poison. Figure out who is on your roster, and then determine why they are there. Finally, ask yourself, "What do I deserve?" and then "What do they deserve?"

The Six Who Carry Your Casket

In this book I talk a lot about being conscious of the people who are around you. In the section *Stop Getting Drunk and High*, I talked about removing poisonous people and behaviors from your life. In the section *Who is on your roster?*, I spoke about building the right team and network. I talked about adding value to people's lives as well as making sure they do the same for you.

Let's talk about that a little bit more. I have had the honor of being a pallbearer three times in my life. Each time it meant something different to me. Being a pallbearer for my grandmother was the toughest and hardest of them all. The reason is that she had been there for me through some of the hardest times in my life. She guided and supported me when I felt like I had nobody.

There are six people who will physically drop your casket into your grave. I'm sure you don't want any random six people to carry you; it should be six people who matter. I was honored to carry her casket and lead her into the church for her funeral, while my cousin Jason was right on my side and my uncle somewhere in the mix as well.

It is vital to understand the distinct difference between your roster and the six people I am referring to here. For example, I currently have an editor who will edit this book for me; I have a barber who makes me sexy and a chiropractor who works on my spinal alignment. I have a psychologist who makes me think, a workout partner who keeps me in shape, and then I have a business coach who gives me lessons on money. These people are part of my roster.

Understand that these people are extremely important. As a matter of fact, I have to replace my dentist because the guy is a jerk and only wants me to do procedures that increase his revenue but do not focus on my goals. He is getting cut from my roster and will never be on my roster again. He does not deserve to be on my team. Are you hearing what I'm saying to you?

The six are different. Not only will they carry your casket, but they will also carry you during life. The six should consist of people you love, cherish, and cannot live without. The six people in your life who are most influential, important, and treasured need to be loved by you.

This book focuses on what you can do to amplify, capitalize on, and dictate your goals, life, and behaviors. This book will help you with your goals and more. Still, it is critically important that you invest time, love, and concern for these six people. Remember that being successful is easier when you live in love. So, it is crucial to develop the love you need in life. I encourage you to identify at least six people you can call right now. Let them know how much you appreciate them, how much they mean to you, and the reason why your relationship exists.

In an earlier chapter, I referenced the importance of understanding the reason *why* you do what you do. It is super important that you identify, contact, and show appreciation to these people so they can be a part of what you do. Do not make this a one-time occurrence. Contribute to and add value to these people's lives today, right now, and then set a reminder to do it again in thirty days. It is your duty to add value to people's lives. You want success, right? You want to get what you deserve, right? Then, you need to give. Who better to give to than the people who are going to carry your casket?

I have some of the biggest goals and aspirations of anyone I know; however, I, like you, need to improve on this particular behavior. It is not fair to people around you if you do not tell them how much you appreciate them, let them know how much you value them, and how their efforts are irreplaceable. Six is just a target; it can be more or less. However, appreciating and showing thanks and gratitude are behaviors we need to engage in more. Listen, 80 percent of people quit their job because they do not like their boss. That's an alarming statistic. But what if your boss was sincere and showed you how much he or she appreciated your efforts? I'd bet my salary that if your boss showed you how much he or she cared about your efforts, you'd work harder and not quit. Think about it like this: if you were to plant a tree and water it and give it sunlight, it would grow. Assume that you are a tree and your flowers, branches, and leaves are going to blossom. My question to you is this: Have you ever seen one tree sprout up and grow naturally? No, typically there are a bunch of trees around each other. So, be mindful that once you grow and grow the others around you, you will wake up and see a jungle of trees (people like you, around you). Do not be selfish and plant only your tree; make sure you are planting, shedding light on, and watering these other people so that you'll look back on your life and see a jungle and not just an individual tree. Give thanks. Do not wait for Thanksgiving or a birthday. If you have employees, a partner, or children, let them know right now that you appreciate them. If they are the six who will carry your casket, then do it often.

Never Worry About Your Competition

People always say you need to compare or benchmark yourself off someone else's success. For example, if you are the number two or three salesperson in your industry, your managers will tell you to do this or that to achieve the status that number one has.

In relationships, you'll notice thousands of attractive people who look way better than you do, who could sexually please your partner better than you can, and who could make them happier.

In parenting, you may notice your best friend works fifteen fewer hours than you do, and he or she uses time wisely in order to spend more time at home with the children.

All three settings are the same, and nothing changes but the way you define it. Your perception of each situation will determine the "way it is." For example, if you want the best relationship, the most profitable job, or a rewarding parent-child relationship, there is one thing that you must do: you must never ever worry about your competition.

I can't express to you enough the value of not worrying about the competition. Once you compare yourself to what everyone else is doing, you throw away your innovative ability. Being conscious of your opponents' results and actions may benefit you, but the real power is in staying in your lane and focusing on you.

Once you move into the mode of acceleration, you do not have time to compare yourself to your competition. I am a writer, an author, and a salesperson. I will be in sales my whole life. I will be a writer as long as I have the cognitive ability to produce. In my mind, I am the best, and will be the best writer who exists. I'm humble, and I understand that there are writers who are regarded as immortal. As of today, I am not one of them; however, I am 100 percent convinced that I will be one of them.

Remember when I was talking about finding the *why* you do things, and what is your motivating factor? One of my motivating factors is my name. Have you ever seen the movie *Troy* featuring Brad Pitt and Eric Baan? The opening scene is worded so magically; it captures the essence of what it means to be motivated by your name. This is the opening line:

Men are haunted by the vastness of eternity, and so we ask ourselves: Will our actions echo across the centuries? Will strangers hear our names long after we are gone, and wonder who we were, how bravely we fought, how fiercely we loved?

Damn, when I wrote that, I got chills. Your name, too, will live on. Think about how you talk about a loved one who is no longer here.

In the movie's opening lines, a young boy hands Achilles, a Greek god played by Brad Pitt, his shield and sword and says, "The soldier you are fighting is the biggest man I've ever seen. I wouldn't want to fight him." Pitt responds, "That's why no one will remember your name." Then he rides off on a horse into the battle.

This scene purely represents why knowing your motivating factor and never worrying about your competition are vital components to success. It does not matter that he was fighting one of the greatest warriors of the day, and, truthfully, why should it matter? So he can allow fear, judgment, and doubt to set in?

In not worrying about competition, it's especially important in your love life that you never, ever worry about the competition. If your significant other was out at the bar and approached by a person a lot more attractive than you are, would you be worried right now? If the answer is yes, then you have not fulfilled your duty and responsibility in the relationship. For the sake of killing the competition, increase your acceleration and effort levels in order to make your spouse think of you any time these situations arise. Let your spouse know not just before he or she goes out, but all the time. Remind that person of the reason why you two are together. Talk about your dreams and goals together. Increase the number of hugs, kisses, and special things you do for that person, starting right now.

Most of us are selfish lovers, and we need to stop that. We need to give way more. We need to give twice as much as we take from our relationship. We need to put more into the bank of love than we take out of that account, and we need our love account to be positive. If your account is positive, you will not have to worry about the competition, nor will you have to worry about doubt and infidelity. You will spend so much time being in love and exuding love that you will not have time to worry about the other people your spouse could be entertaining in his or her free time. Remember, like I said in the effort and attitude chapter, you cannot control another person. The only thing you can control is your effort and attitude. With that being understood, take control of your effort and attitude by killing the competition with your acceleration—and not with your constant worrying about the competition.

No matter what aspect of your life needs improvement, this mind-set is common to all of them. In your business or in your relationships, never worry about the competition. Worry instead about how you can change, evolve, and innovate. Worry about what you can improve, enhance, and make better. Focus on what adds love to your love account, money to your bank account, and bliss to your nirvana account. You are better than you were a year ago; you deserve bliss and all the success that you want to create.

8. YOU SHOULD BE AND STAY PISSED OFF

Everyone responds to adversity differently, but the only way you should respond is with concentrated anger. The only time I will ever tell you to harvest a feeling that could, subjectively, be deemed negative is right now. You should always harness the anger felt from something not going your way as motivation to drive you toward a goal.

I got kicked out of college after being on academic probation and obtaining passing grades. How does that even happen? Due to inconsistencies in the system and a lack of explanation from my athletic academic advisor, I took the wrong classes at the wrong time. As a result, years of work went down the drain. My dream of becoming one of the best players at my college was gone; the title of college football player that I earned as a walk-on was gone. I cried. I threw a clock through my wall and cursed everyone around me. I was beyond angry; I was at the highest level of irritation, fury, and indignation. I had just signed a year-long lease and had no income, no car, and now no school to attend at twenty years of age. I had to wake up and deal with the embarrassment, rejection, and ridicule. I couldn't even tell my family and friends at home.

Initially, I was pissed off. I stayed pissed off, and I deserved to stay pissed off. Look, only someone with a negative mind-set will label this situation as negative. It was not negative or positive; it was only what happened. Actually, this was exactly what I created and could have avoided if I would have been operating at the speed of light and not at the speed of the side streets. I deserved to lose my roster spot. I deserved to get kicked out of college, and I deserved to be in a position where I had no income.

You are probably dealing with some type of adversity similar to the situation I just described, but no matter. There is a way out. That clock that I told you about remained in the wall, cord dangling, with paint chips speckled all over the floor.

It took maybe four or five hours before I moved toward acceleration. I contacted a local junior college and asked if I could transfer my university credits to obtain an associate of science degree. I was enrolled that day. I submitted over thirty applications to jobs in a very short time frame. I was willing to take any opportunity I could get; I even had my friend help me fill them out since all applications at that time were paper based. My best friend at the time was a girl whose goals aligned with mine. She was focused on making money and moving forward in school. I was fortunate enough to get a ride with her every day to my classes, sometimes having to stay at the school up to five and six hours because I had no ride. I utilized my time wisely. For example, while she was in class, I would write in my notebooks. I would work out every day, and I would focus on my scholastics. My coach stayed in contact with me and wanted me back on the team, so I stayed focused and knew that I would be back in football soon with the right amount of effort.

The entire time I stayed pissed off, I was a miserable person to be around, but I was so focused on creating a life of bliss where I could do what I wanted that I did not have time for anything that might decelerate me. I did not have time for poisonous people. When I tell you to stay pissed off, I don't mean stay pissed off at life and blame other people. What I mean is, you must use this energy as motivation. You can and will persevere through every obstacle; you just have to believe and stay focused.

During this period, I had the opportunity to turn to drugs, alcohol, or laziness, but I did not allow myself to be a victim. At this time, I had no relationship with my father and had started to resent my mother. In other words, nothing was going right for me; yet, *everything* was going right.

I got a job working at Wal-Mart. I just Google-mapped my apartment and realized it was only three and a half miles away. I would walk that distance any time I did not have a ride. Yes, I walked seven miles just to make the money to pay my rent. I never complained about it; I just did it knowing I had no other option at the time. So, what is your excuse? Get pissed off and go for your goals. You deserve bliss and success.

9. WALK ON TO THE TEAM

I walked on to the football team in college at Northern Illinois University, which is a division one program in the Mid-American Conference. I am not a division one athlete, and I did not earn a scholarship out of high school. I really had no business being on the roster, but I earned it and I created it.

Look, the only reason why walking on to a football team is relative to you is that you have desires, dreams, or a way of life that you want to create but do not currently have. Yet, you have to create a way to get there. I'm assuming you are looking for a management position, creating a business, or trying to lock down your ideal mate for marriage. If you are already married, you are still auditioning for that role. If you want your business to succeed, then behave like someone who walks on to a team. If your responsibility is to drive sales, or you have a burning desire to increase the love in your relationship, you have to think like a walk-on.

Have you ever seen the movie *Rudy,* the movie about the guy who is too slow, too small, and not athletic enough to be on the Notre Dame football roster? There are only a few movies that make me cry, but this is one of them First of all, my life was similar to his. And my life, honestly, is probably no different from yours. Correct me if I am wrong, but I'm sure we both have desires; we want to win, and we probably have had a little bit of doubt or fear, whether it be internal or from external sources. A walk-on embraces life like this: "Look, nobody is going to give me a fair shot. Nobody is going to create a job for me, and nobody is going to make my relationship great." A walk-on knows that he or she is not entitled to anything. He or she has not created enough attention and will not have the same access to opportunity as the players on scholarship.

In my case, I knew that at any moment, if I did not put forth enough effort and consistency toward my workouts, I would not be good enough to get on and stay on the team. This is the way you have to approach life. Do not assume that anything is certain. Assume that you have to earn your spot every day; complacency is not an option. It is not normal to feel entitled to anything. What makes you so great that you're entitled to a spot? Humble yourself enough to realize that if you do not bust your ass every day toward your goals, then you do not deserve them. Walk-ons know that they have the ability to create the same results as the scholarship players. As a walk-on, you have to be what is called a "try-hard." Yes, these players get made fun of all the time—you know, those people who try way too hard in all settings, situations, and moments? Well, you need to be a try-hard all the time. Do not allow one of the prima donnas to convince you to decrease your efforts because of the environment. Impose your damned will on your obstacles; impose your will on your goals and competition. Nobody can be as great as you when you accept that you are amazing. You have the power to do anything you set your mind to, so impose your will every day.

Look, your goal should be to try so hard that you attract the name "try-hard." Your effort needs to be so high that you earn a spot on the team every day. With the walk-on mentality, you are a person who will show up to a place and create opportunity. You will take an opportunity instead of expecting something to be handed to you. When adversity strikes and things do not go your way, you have to impose your will; you have to think like a walk-on. You have to think, "I deserve this spot and I need it. I cannot live without it."

10. Add More Value than Anyone Else

People are always asking, "How can I lose weight?" and "How can I get a million dollars?" and "How can I improve my relationships, bank account, or life?" If you have kids, I'm sure you want your children to be great contributors to society, smart, and happy. I'm sure you want them to be healthy and have healthy relationships. If you are an entrepreneur, I'm sure you want your business to grow, your income to increase, and your name to carry weight in your community. If you are a student-athlete, I'm sure you want to meet and excel in the classroom as well as break all the records at your given school and drive them to a championship. What I am saying is this: your realm does not matter. One factor alone will propel you far beyond the competition. Improve yourself day after day, and ensure that you accelerate toward your dreams and goals.

Be the person who brings the most value to any given situation. In sport video games, the players are based on real-life players and are given attribute ratings based on the players' real-life abilities. These ratings determine how the computer-animated system will predict their behavior in the game. In a competition, you typically want to pick the team or set of players that give you the best chance to win the game. For example, in the legendary Madden franchise, historically I have played with a quarterback whose accuracy attribute is in the top 1 percent of the game. Why? I feel like I need to reduce the risk of fluky video-game tactics that I cannot control, and since my personal plan of attack is to cover the most yards in the shortest amount of time, I need a quarterback with a very accurate arm. I often pick teams like the Patriots for Tom Brady or a Manning brother's team. All are great and none is really better than the other, just relative to what type of performance I want. Look at your smartphone; it has attributes as well. Some have large screens, better battery, and faster processors. Some smartphones sync better with your equipment, or they make it easy for you to text message or stay connected. Now you get the point I am trying to make. Everything that exists comes with a certain number of attributes.

If we measured human attributes on a scale of one to ten, and then we looked at all of a person's possible attributes, we would obtain an overall rating. Some categories might include the following: communication skills, motivation, critical thinking ability, adaptability, and determination. Of course, this is hypothetical because nobody ranks us on a trading card; however, understand that these attributes do in fact exist in our society, and people are always judging us. The higher your attribute ranking, the higher your relationship, your business, and your life. Don't believe me?

Value matters. Value is a key to success. How much value do you bring to a person's life? How much value are you bringing to your company? How much value do you have in your relationship? We have to understand that we are unique; we are one, and nobody is like us on this planet. The attributes we choose to amplify are the ones that will drive us into the lane of success. Going back to the Madden rating system, there are quarterbacks who possess high overall ratings but do not perform well throwing short, accurate passes because they're athletic running quarterbacks. On the other hand, some quarterbacks are amazingly accurate but are immobile and get sacked a lot. Why does this matter to you? Awareness is king, and knowing what your highest and lowest attributes are will determine how much and how well you bring value to the table.

Picture a judge in the highest court of the land, lauded for his or her in-depth knowledge and great understanding of the legal system. At the same time, this person is impatient, does not listen well, and jumps to conclusions all too often. From a knowledge standpoint, you would give him or her the highest score, nine out of nine. But the judge's overall ranking would suffer due to his or her lack of patience and poor listening skills.

Friends, my point is this: these types of people are rampant in our society. We live in a time where consciousness and awareness of one's presence is lacking and misunderstood; we live in a land of no identity. Do not be one of these people; do not join the sheep and the non-thinking. Reach far above the status quo and understand, acknowledge, and embrace what you are. Knowing your values is a key to success, and knowing how you bring that value is key to the success of others around you. Nothing moves without value. If you want to have enough food in your refrigerator, you'd better start adding value to people's lives who can hand you the money.

Deliver the Most Value Every Time

Ten percent of the battle is listed on the preceding pages— knowing your value, understanding how you can use it, and understanding it relative to the entire entity that is you. Highlight, underline, and quote me on this. One of the biggest responsibilities you have on Earth is to deliver the most value to every situation, every time, with every person. Delivering value is what separates the accelerated from everyone else. This applies to the simplest and smallest facet of life.

Think back to your favorite teacher from school, your favorite television show growing up, or even your current best friend. Remember the chapter about knowing and understanding the *why*? Well, why are these memories so easily connected? I can tell you that I loved the "Mighty Morphine Power Rangers" because of the drama. My favorite teacher was Mrs. Christiansen because she was gorgeous. And my best friend always questions me and makes me think critically about life.

Now, in each of those instances, although the value was different, these are things I cannot forget. In relationships, in business, or as a parent or teacher, you have to apply this to your own behavior and product. You have to create things that are unforgettable. The only way to create and deliver on a product, service, or relationship that is unforgettable is to deliver the most value every time. Remember, you are a product. When you go to church, for example, and you interact with the other patrons, not only are they watching how you deliver or under deliver; they are watching your kids. The staff and your god are watching you. How much value are you bringing every week? When you go to the practice field and your football, baseball, or basketball team underperforms, and you, being one of the best players, do not go as hard as you can in practice, you wonder why? They are watching your behavior and performance all the time. If you are the manager of a retail location, and your store fails to reach quota, fails to maintain a solid customer base, or fails to yield profits, assume that you are not bringing enough value to the table. Finally, in the relationship setting with your significant other, the only way to make it work forever, the only way for it to be rewarding and to make both of you happy, is to bring as much value to the situation as possible every time, over and over.

What are the benefits of adding value?

Adding value is the secret, the key, the trick to get everything you want. To gain, you must give (sacrifice). If you give at an accelerated rate that moves at the speed of light, you will attract others who want to give to you, who want to support you, and who want to believe in your dream. Remember, what you do does not matter—only *why* and *how* you do it. So, if you want to be rich, then you need to act rich and bring more value to the opportunities that will make you rich. When your scale of value is so high that it cannot be measured, you won't even have to worry about the competition. As I said before, the competition will not exist because you will be the only option. You have to convince yourself that by adding value to a person, it will improve what is weak; the concern is an area of opportunity.

Let's focus on relationships and typical relationship settings. In today's world, people suffer from a lack of identity, and everyone is jostling for a position to stand out or fit in. What's more, most people do not even know what they are striving for. I am writing this book in the age of information, the technology age. In this age, traditional gender roles have been questioned due to increased activity in women's rights and civil rights. I wanted to keep this book timeless; however, it is important for me to address the constant change and expectation prevalent in our society. Because we are starting to accept each other regardless of our differences, we are becoming a society that strives to depend less, desire less, and want less from other people. Do not get foolish and think that you can do this on your own. Because of all the recent changes, people feel empowered to do everything alone, without help from or respect for anyone else. Look, I'm here to break the news to you. No person can reach amazing, world-changing, life-impacting results without help from others. You have to attract people who are not poisonous, who benefit you, and who deserve things the same way you do.

What are the major benefits of adding value? Empowerment, growth, and trust building. I use this quote often: "Find where you can add value before you abuse what you can take." Most good-hearted people will give you every dollar they have and every bit of advice they have. That being said, it's crucial that you do not abuse that ability. The world is selfish. In fact, a selfish person will read this book about acceleration and success and think this book is a mandate to "take." You are guaranteed that it is a mandate to take, an order and a commandment that you are required to accelerate your life. I just do not want a selfish, narrow-minded person to think that this means continue on in your selfish ways. Successful people bring more to the table than anyone else, and this is how they become successful. If you want success, then you must bring more value than everyone, every time. You want your presence to be so grand and strong that everyone can win and gain from what you have.

A woman who is insecure because of her past relationships or her body image will become secure first when she decides to be secure and second when another person adds value to her by letting her know that nothing is wrong with her, that she is beautiful just the way she is. Be that person.

A student who is struggling to pass a class or some level of academic success will succeed when he or she decides to; however, you can grow, empower, and accelerate that person by letting him or her know that you believe in his or her work ethic. Be that student, or support that student.

An underperforming employee, due to laziness, can be accelerated by simply having a realistic conversation with him or her. You can accelerate a person by adding value to that person's experience, knowledge, and overall attribute rating. Be that person. Add more to your work environment.

If you work on commission or you're an entrepreneur or are thinking of selling a new product, master the value of that product so you can connect it to the right customer. Be the salesperson you are cut out to be.

Everything that exists on this planet has a quota, an expectation, and needs to be accelerated at the speed of light in order to be successful and worth the investment.

11.SUCCESS IS EVERY NIGHT, NOT OVER NIGHT

Once you decide that success is the only thing you want to create, a flow of energy will permeate your mind, body, and soul unlike anything you've ever experienced. The attraction of success is one of the most powerful magnets in the universe. Have you ever wondered why winners keep winning? Most people who become champions are repeat champions. Winning is contagious.

Michael Jordan and his Bulls won six championships; Kobe's Lakers won five. Look at Phil Jackson and John Wooden, who both won ten plus championships. What about *Ben-Hurl*, *Titanic*, and *The Lord of the Rings* "The Return of the King," all of which scored eleven Academy Awards? Success is a culture, an expectation, and a lifestyle. What about Walt Disney who earned twenty-two Oscars? The New York Yankees have to date twenty-seven world championships, and the Lakers and Celtics have sixteen plus.

I have to pay my respect to the grandfather of self-help and improvement, Napoleon Hill. His book *Think and Grow Rich* was originally published in 1937, during the Great Depression. It has sold over seventy million copies.

Winning, success, and acceleration at their finest are about reproducing, duplicating, and repeating success over and over. The word that comes to mind is *consistency*. Bring consistency and value to the table every day. Success at this level solves all your current problems. Success at this level will create a sustained nirvana that is orgasmic. When you reach the activity levels at the speed of light, your acceleration is so grand that you haven't the time for things that do not generate more money, a better relationship, or better overall health.

A healthy relationship, a bank account full of money, and children who go out and become leaders are all created by your commitment to one idea, the idea that *success is every night, not overnight*. Understand that consistency is required to become successful.

Look at your bank account; it does one of two things. It either accepts withdrawals or it makes deposits. Keep in mind that withdrawals are deceleration-type activities at the fullest, and acceleration is deposit after deposit after deposit. In the relationship realm, you have to make deposit after deposit over and over, every day. You have to go above and beyond expectation every day. Reinvent yourself in the relationship; send your partner flowers, candy, and thank-you cards. You need to grow your partner every single day. Make sure that person knows he or she is appreciated. Show that person how much you love and desire his or her time. There is no way a half-ass commitment or half-ass behaviors will make your deposits and account enormous. Let's make a deposit every single day. This is not a game; this is your life.

What about your business or your athletic reach? How can you be successful? How can you have maximum acceleration? How can you do anything successfully if you do not decide that you DESERVE it?

<u>Why give up?</u>

I don't understand why some people give up so easily when they are reaching for a goal. In high school, with no playing time as a junior, I knew I was going to have a career after college. I was so convinced that I was the best football player in my high school at the time, yet I couldn't even get on the field. I wanted to give up and quit. I felt like my effort was not appreciated and that I was worthless. At the same time, I knew that this plan to play college football was going to work. I knew that I had to up my level of effort and invest in myself. While my teammates were leaving every day to go to lunch at Wendy's and McDonald's, I stayed at the high school. I stayed there on my lunch breaks because I needed to watch films; I needed to watch football, sleep in football, and drown in it. I knew that I did not know enough about football. I knew that in order for me to accelerate, I was required to change my behaviors and create activities that increased my football value. I did not make it on to the field because I did not bring enough value. In sports, the worst behavior is to quit. In the movie *Rudy*, which is based on the life of a Notre Dame walk-on football player, Rudy never quit. He never gave up.

12. GUARD YOURSELF AT ALL TIMES

Nearly fifteen thousand people gathered at the MGM Grand Casino in Las Vegas, Nevada, on a September night in 2011. The crowd watched in awe as Floyd May weather returned from his hiatus to dominate the first three rounds of a fight with up-and-coming boxer Victor Ortiz. At the time, May weather was undefeated and one of the biggest cash cows in the world. He had accelerated the sport of boxing so much that, based on a relative comparison to other boxing eras, he *is* boxing. He is without a doubt the face of boxing, the best boxer in his class, and maybe the pound-for-pound best fighter, after Mike Tyson. May weather's work ethic and results keep him at the speed of light, accelerating at all times, which, as we now know, is required for success, growth, and happiness.

This fight goes down as one of the most poetic events to ever occur in a sport; it's poetry so strong and deep that we all need to learn from it and apply the lesson to our day-to-day life. Acceleration occurs when you move forward. Even while moving forward, you will come across some type of conflict, force, or restriction that will try to hold you back from victory. Some obstacles will be in the form of friends, spouses, or family, and some will be legal. There are rules in a boxing match, and throwing a head-butt at your opponent, for example, violates the rules, calling for an immediate deduction for the fighter accused of the action. Ortiz was guilty of that on this night. With Floyd backed into a corner he jolted upward with his head toward May weather. The skull, containing the strongest bone in our body, the cranium, is a dangerous weapon, especially when acceleration plus a lack of anticipation occurs. If you are able to jar the other person's head violently enough, it can kill him or her. Well, after the head-butt, the ref stopped the fight to separate the two. Once the fight resumed, in just a split second history was made. Floyd stayed on guard; he kept his defense and offense ready to go. While Ortiz was worried about May weather's opinion of him and was looking to apologize and make it right, Floyd made it right, pun intended. He struck Ortiz, knocking him out for the victory—a payday of over twenty-five million dollars and more controversy to add to his legacy. A lesson indeed.

Guard Up

You do not deserve to let your guard down. This is a world full of threats, danger, and competition. No matter what lane you choose, from business to athletics to relationships, you are required to be ready to defend or offend at all times. You should always be ready to defend your work, your dream, and your plan.

If you are married or plan to be, what you have to understand is that when you go out, run errands, or attend events, there is always that chance of someone trying to steal your heart. You have to accelerate and guard your relationship; you can't let your partner down. The dream you two have of growing, traveling, and winning together comes only when both people are able to fight off all distractions. You have no chance to win the championship if you do not keep your guard up.

In business, I want to quote philosopher Lil Wayne: "Yeah, too much money isn't enough money." No matter your type of business, growth matters, money matters, and growing the amount of money you have matters. Set really high destinations, and then guard the money dream at all costs. You should require yourself to grow, obtain, and multiply your income as often as possible. While I was writing this book, one of the businesses that I mentor doubled its income by simply accepting acceleration. A personal training business from Chicago was able to secure more clients and new opportunities in fewer than thirty days by simply changing the destination, curbing the amount of effort exerted, and expecting acceleration at all levels. The company's founder said to me on the phone, "Now I see what I am worth." Doubling your income is easy, but it starts with thought followed by protecting your dream every single day. Remember, success is not over night; it's every night. You literally have to fight every day to obtain the amount of money that you desire.

Your life will change so much that you will have to ground yourself in your core values. May weather proved that guarding yourself at all times can cost you millions of dollars; it can cost you the advantages of good health plus the legacy you plan to create. If the outcome had been the other way around, what would have been the ramifications for Floyd? A smaller paycheck, an injured jaw, and a legacy that would have been tarnished? In less than one second, a career could have been changed. This is why it is so important that you accelerate at all times, you defend your dreams at all times.

Defending your dream is not solely about playing defense. And please understand what I mean when I say "defend." In football you have three sides of the ball. You have the offense, defense, and special team players. Collectively, their goal is to win the game by scoring more points than the opponent. Life is about winning; you want your partner to be happy, a job that is rewarding, and health that will allow you to play with the kids. Life is about being able to do nothing with someone you love, and having it mean everything. Life is about that moment when you see your kids off to college, or when they come home with their first child. Life is about that moment you make your first five-thousand-dollar paycheck, you open your doors to your business, or you make that first sale as an entrepreneur. Life is about accelerating at the speed of light, going so fast and fierce that everything and everyone who gets in your way is liable to get stung by your energy. Defending your dream is important. It's so important that it does not matter if you want to look at it like a football team on the offense, trying to score over and over and over again. That method will work, and the more you shoot, the more you score. Keep putting up attempts because they will go in, and you will win. Defense is the same way. You can guard, defend, and protect my dreams, my acceleration, my health, and wealth with the same amount of fearlessness with which you attack. There is no difference. Protect your dreams, your life, your family, your wealth, and your health at all times.

13. THE DRAKE EFFECT

When you create art, you want to create art that is timeless—at least, this is what I was told. In the age of technology, however, your art needs to be relevant. This is why I wanted to write a chapter about the musician Drake. For those of you who will read this long after we are dead and gone, the age in which we live is dominated by hip-hop music, which generally comes from artists from the inner city who exploit their city's corruption, culture, and violence through novel expressions of creativity. In hip-hop, there is a certain rule, expectation, and belief that masculinity is the most dominate, important, and attractive trait to an artist who endeavors to become successful. Hip-hop itself has been all about competition, from B-boy break-dance battles, to freestyle dis battles, to record sales. The Drake Effect is a term I use to refer to Drake's success, how he created it, and what we can learn from it. In the effort to become and stay accelerated, we have to cross-train our brains to learn from other people's experiences and success. There are formulas in every success story that we can apply to our daily lives.

Drake, first of all, does not look like a rapper. He is a skinny, light-skinned, well-spoken actor who followed his passion for music. Drake is the epitome of success. In 2009 he had all the major record labels bidding for his talent. His first two CDs went platinum, meaning he sold over one million copies, which is an industry standard for success. He has been touring and doing features nonstop for the last four or five years. He's made over twenty million dollars in the last two years respectively. Drake could walk into any place in America and be recognized right now; this is success. His music will live forever and, most important, the Drake Effect has created, changed, and altered music as we know it. His music has changed people's behaviors, the way they dress, and the way they think about each other. His poetry resonates deep within people who have had turbulent relationships.

Why is the Drake Effect important to you? From this brief explanation of hip-hop and Drake's success, we can extract three main principles to apply in any situation. Remember, I said that cross-training our brain matters, so let's look at it. Although only you can determine what success is and where you choose to apply the acceleration mind-set, all efforts toward success require the same amount of focus. Obtaining good grades, graduating college, becoming an entrepreneur, starting a family, becoming fit, writing a book, and traveling the world require the same amount of focus, for example. Use these three Drake principles to create the wealth, health, and bliss you deserve: blatant objectivity, knowing your target, and believing in the dream.

14.BLATANT OBJECTIVITY

What the hell is blatant objectivity, and why does it matter? It matters because it is literally the sole difference in understanding what, where, and how you need to improve to obtain whatever you desire. Blatant objectivity means being as honest as possible with yourself and with everyone around you. It is one of the biggest and most important attributes that one must possess in order to obtain, create, and maintain success. In keeping with the title, I want to provide a few of Drake's lyrics with an explanation of them, as they paint a perfect picture of the notion of blatant objectivity. The following lyrics are from a powerful song he created in 2009 called "The Calm":

Feeling' so distant from everyone I've known, to make everybody happy I think I would need a clone…I'm sitting in a chair, but in the future it's a throne…life is so insane, look what I've became, trying to make a name…they love it when you smile, unaware that it's a strain.

This is the type of honesty that I love and appreciate. It actually means something to us. People like me and you have to be honest like this with ourselves. What do these lyrics mean, and why do they matter to us? What he is saying here is this: at the time he was striving for and trying to create success, he got so overwhelmed and absorbed in his projects that everyone he used to know just became a distant figure. Everyone in this life wants something from him, and there was no way he could please everyone, including himself, with the little bit of time he had. He makes fun of life because all he is trying to do is create his legacy, and now it's a crazy turnaround from what it used to be. He also speaks about the faces he has to put on. In other words, you have to smile, but it's not always easy because of the pain, loneliness, and misunderstanding.

This matters to all of us because we are going to stumble, fall, and want to quit in our quest for success. I do not care what anyone tells you; it's not easy to create all the things you want to create in life. I know how hard it can be for the simplest things to happen and go right. It usually takes a lot more energy and effort than people can comprehend. I'll be honest with you. My day-to-day sales are sometimes a struggle, and I can get de-motivated. But I have an amazing recovery that allows me to refocus. *The Accelerated* is your guide to help you refocus.

I'm trying my best to accept myself for who I am today and create a lane of wealth and health for my family. During my writing of this book, people I do not even know are motivating me to work hard every day, and it is hard. It's challenging. I want to make my wife the happiest woman on the planet and to create success so my children will be whatever they desire. But I struggle. I know this book is telling you to keep focused, move forward, and accelerate, and I want you to know from the bottom of my heart that I struggle, too. I have areas of opportunities and deficiencies as well. I believe that through writing I have the ability to help, impact, and improve people's lives. I want you to know that blatant objectivity matters and that you should always be looking at yourself holistically, as if you were a fly on the wall observing everything. Without bias or judgment, you must understand who you are and the situations you are in. I speak about success because I have created it, and I live in a mind-set that only allows me to think of success. I came from a much worse place, though. If I do not stay focused, I will falter and spiral into a life of addiction, fallacies, and negativity. I urge you to be fully honest with yourself and your situations, the people around you, and the beliefs you have. Once you can look at yourself, then you can make massive changes or strides. But you have to be honest; it is necessary for success. If I was an alcoholic, do you think I would do well as a bartender? Well, maybe yes because I know the product, but I wouldn't be able to sustain the income I need because I would likely spend most of it as it's coming in. What about a guy who wants to get good grades but never studies, never puts time in at the library, and has poor attendance in class? How successful is that person going to be? What about the guy who wants to make a million dollars but refuses to think outside the box of his day-to-day job? How are you going to be a millionaire if the only thing you do is go to work? Finally, what about the manager who wants his or her team to succeed but puts himself or herself above the team and blames them for everything? You need blatant objectivity to succeed, to identify problems, and to view your life—blueprint and plan—so you can grow it and get what you deserve.

15. TARGETS AND BELIEVING

Knowing Your Target

You will have multiple struggles; you will have setbacks; and you will want to give up more than once. Since you are accelerated, you won't quit; you won't give up; and you won't back down. But the problems that will surface mean nothing. What matters most is your target. You have to know your target, and you have to focus on it and attract it. Dream chasing is fun, but we do not chase dreams. We are the accelerated. We attract and create dreams. We create what we want with specific thoughts and then actions over actions. Like I stated before, I've dealt with doubt, loneliness, and I've always struggled with accepting myself as I am. It comes from a fear of feeling inadequate. No matter what actions I'd take, I used to feel as if they were not good enough. Blatant objectivity is OK; see, I am not assigning meaning to any of what I just said. Remember how I talked about assigning meaning to things? Slow down with the meaning assignment. Just because these are the things I'm struggling with does not mean something is wrong, negative, or bad. They are just things that *are*, and I will not allow them to diminish my happiness, output, or income—and neither should you.

What matters, and what you have to remind yourself of every

day, is your target and who you are targeting. My target is to create a legacy. I want people to hear my name and associate it with success, which they already do but not on the scale I deserve. I want people to know that I truly care about creating, showing, and sacrificing to help people improve. I have a special talent that allows me to take a leadership role in every environment. I have a talent that allows me to figure out how to motivate people and, more importantly, it is my desire. It is fun. I get a thrill and I am at bliss when I am able to influence, help, and motivate people to improve. Yes, I want to be a best-selling author but, more importantly, as I mentioned in the first chapter of this book, I deserve it. You, your family, and your dream deserve you to become accelerated, to stay accelerated, and to never lose sight of your target. Creating a target allows you to understand the direction, effort, and energy required to achieve. For example, have you noticed the recent trend of weight loss shakes and products being sold? Our country has a high obesity rate, and people are trying to seize the capital opportunities at hand. Let's look at this trend as if you were on either side of this, either as a person attempting to lose weight or as a person who wanted to be an agent of change for the people who were losing weight. You have to KNOW YOUR TARGET. If you are trying to lose weight, then you need to find a gym, a trainer, a nutritionist, a dietician, a support system, a workout partner, a blog, and a book or a DVD that will support you in your efforts. As someone who wants to lose weight, you have two targets: the target of losing weight and the target of the people, companies, and resources that are going to help you. On the opposite side, you are an agent of change, and your job is to assist these people to lose weight. Your job, then, is to know your target and find these people. Knowing your target and your target audience matters. It is crucial to your success. When Drake makes music, he is very aware that he is making music for young women in their teens or twenties, at least at this point. Women in this age group are the most emotionally sensitive creatures that exist. In doing this he is a genius; he makes sure his music relates to their struggles. The result has been millions of dollars, providing him with the financial security that many of you are striving for. You can do it. You just have to know your target and deliver on what they deserve.

Believing in the Dream

Believing in the dream is the last principle of the Drake Effect, the one that starts in your mind, the one that starts with a thought and will send all the energy you need to succeed into the universe.

You have to believe in your dream, no matter what happens to you. You have to believe that the outcome that you deserve will occur after you take the right actions over and over. Remember that Drake did not fit the mold of success in his field. He was not a typical rapper. He was told he would not make it; he was laughed at and mocked over and over again by peers and fans. That is the price of success, my friends. Success comes with criticism, doubt, and people who will have an opinion about you.

You have to roll with the punches to survive. I know that I will endure criticism from those who believe I have no writing ability, no talent, and they will call me arrogant because I am crazy enough to actually think that I can impact the world for good. I do not care about any of that. I only care about the hours that turned into years of my perfecting my craft and becoming an excellent writer. I care about the thousands of dollars I just invested to travel to desolate, uncivilized places so I could write this book and tap into an inner level of peace and understanding. I care about the fact that I'm sacrificing sleep or time away from my friends and family to fulfill my dream. I'm sacrificing my Memorial Day weekend to sit in a dark room and write until I cannot write anymore, while my peers are out at the beach, at clubs, and at barbecues. You have to believe in the dream, regardless of what party weekend it may be. When a critic says to me, "Don't use references to Drake; make your art timeless, and don't put dates in it because it will limit the number of books you can sell over time," I tell them to jump off a bridge. I believe in my dream, and I do not care about the people who do not. People, I want to transfer this power to you every day. You have to unconditionally believe in your dream, with no reservations.

I laugh, and I use it as motivation. This is my project and my dream, and I am sacrificing everything I need to make it happen. This is what I want you, and the world, to do. We have to sacrifice for our dreams; we have to go in it knowing the finish line and result. We don't need to know what happens in between; we only need to know where we are and where we are going to finish.

Look, you deserve bliss, happiness, and success. You deserve to be loved, to give love, and to live life to the fullest. No matter what these ignorant people say, you have the innate ability to create anything you want. The human mind is incredibly strong, and enhancing its ability by simply believing in its ability to do so is mandatory. Drake said it best before he had musical and financial success: "I want it all; that's why I strive for it. I know that it's coming. I just hope I'm alive for it—I just want to be successful." Muhammad Ali said over and over before he obtained his boxing success that he was the greatest, using self-hypnosis and mental practice to create the lane of success that he deserved. New Year's Eve, 1961, the Beatles arrived at Decca Records so they could audition to get signed as a music group. Guess what? They were rejected and not signed. The move goes down as one of the dumbest moves ever because the Beatles became one of the greatest music groups to ever perform. Regardless of failure, they believed in the dream and believed that they would get what they deserved. Remember, practice blatant objectivity, know your targets, and always believe in your dream.

16.EXECUTION

(NOTE: EXECUTION IS THE NUMBER ONE REASON WHY PEOPLE DON'T ACHIEVE GOALS, EXECUTION IS THE "HOW" IT WILL HAPPEN.)

Acceleration is a high-level understanding of success creation. Everyone wants to be loved and wants to succeed. We all have dreams and goals, but most people have no idea how to create what they truly desire.

The way to achieve your dreams is to learn how to execute them. Most people have no idea how to execute their dreams; most people have a very low expectation of what type of energy is needed to follow through with your dreams.

It's a very simple idea, but it is the main difference between getting your dreams and plans off the page and into your life. Step one is to dream and dream big. Step two is to execute the dream. It starts with the first step, the first phone call, or the first client. When I started collecting data to write my first book, I asked my cousin for advice. Her response was, "Do it." Creating success, health, and wealth is about taking the tools you have and applying consistent action over and over again. Or, as Nike put it, "Just Do It."

Most people believe that all you need is a "plan" to reach your dreams. I'll be the first person to tell you this, and keep in mind I have reached multiple dreams over and over again. It never happens the way you plan it; it always changes and always shifts. The first step of executing is going, doing, or showing up to the party. That is where most people fail because they spend so much time planning and gathering data that they forget that action is required for success. People assume they need to gather all this information and data because it will guarantee their success, forgetting that experience is a better teacher than education. If I start a consignment business today and you start researching it today, once we come together in a year, who will be better off and more advanced? It'll be the person who takes action and risk. The person who is reading will still be reading. I'm not trying to discredit people who want to read, research, and gather data because those activities are a valuable portion of the entire pie in reaching for whatever it is you desire. Still, I am advocating for the person who takes risks, takes action, and gets into the face of their dreams. Here are some steps to help you understand how to execute:

Clearly define the expectation or goal. This will enable you to answer questions about what you want as the final outcome. It will help you assign roles and responsibilities to yourself or the other people invested in this goal. For me, my major goal at this point is to become a best-selling author as quickly as possible. I feel like this is something I deserve, and I should have it tomorrow. Since I have set a defined expectation, I am able to set all my energy, behaviors, and attitude to create that as a reality. Some people consider themselves best sellers based on other people's expectations; however, like we discovered in an earlier chapter, only you can define success. Therefore, the level of sales I want to reach with this book is well beyond what other people expect. I am sharing this personal goal with you because I feel like there is a lot of value in my goal, and I hope that it resonates with you.

Create something consistent. There should be some type of activity that you do over and over that allows you to create consistency. For example, if you want to be a body builder, your first step will be getting into the gym and doing research about how muscle mass grows and develops. Hypothetically, you'd have to create a routine that has you in the gym pumping iron at least four or five times a week. You would have to learn about proteins and carbohydrates; you'd definitely have to change your caloric intake. You would have to keep this up for a week, then a month, then half a year, then a full year, and then at some point you'd realize you are actually a body builder (I'm not saying it takes only a year; I'm just using the example to show consistency). This behavior is exactly what you need to become a body builder. When I wrote this book, I actually had a schedule. My plan was to write this book in fewer than six months. I figured if I would write every day, then it would be down in that time frame. Honestly, I struggled, as I said before. Life happens and that's OK. I've had numerous unexpected issues arise that required my attention. Still, I stayed as consistent as possible. I downloaded an application on my smartphone that would allow me to write down any idea I had, any thought. I created a lane of acceleration where I could focus at any given point and write.

I have a friend who is committed to fitness; she works out five days a week. No matter what happens to her throughout her day, she finds a way to work out. I've never seen anyone commit to a plan the same way she does. Like clockwork, she is at the gym. But the great benefit is that after a while of trying and doing something consistently, it becomes habit. You create a lifestyle change, and it no longer feels like trying. It just feels like life, and it feels easy.

Once you have a plan, be like water and not like brick. Bruce Lee once said

If you try to remember you will lose. Empty your mind; be formless, shapeless, like water. Now you put water into a cup, it becomes the cup. You put water into a teapot, it becomes the teapot. Now water can flow, or creep, or drip or crash. Be water my friend.

Your plan may not go as planned, so you have to figure out another solution. When Heath Ledger played the Joker in *Batman*, one of my favorite quotes was, "Do I really look like a guy with a plan?" The condescending, sarcastic undertone seems to imply that he did not have a plan, when indeed he did. The plan was to terrorize and create massive amounts of chaos in the hearts of Gotham city. When creating a plan to execute your dream, remember what Data from *Star Trek* said about humanity: "The human race has an enduring desire for knowledge and for new opportunities to improve itself."

17.
180 % : THE ACCELRATED COMMITMENT

180 Percent: Accelerated Commitment

It is absolutely mandatory that you reassess your levels of commitment in all avenues of your life. Everything in your life depends on it—your relationship, your education, your fitness, your finances, and your attitude. Look at these areas from a high level of awareness. There are three major factors regarding commitment that I want to share with you, and, trust me, I have struggled with these. Always remember that succeeding and sticking to a commitment is nothing but a choice. The struggle stops when you make that choice, when you make a decision and commit to it. Sales expert Grant Car done says in his book *The 10X Rule*, "Over commit and over deliver. The problem with commitment is that people have so much fear and anxiety about their decisions they cripple up like sardines in a can. My question to you is, where did this fear come from?"

Why do you allow this fear to live inside your soul? Fear is a choice; yet, so many people choose to live in fear, which is why commitment is so hard for people. How many people do you know who have made a New Year's resolution to get back in the gym, but you never see them in the gym after the second week of the year? If you are one of these people, tell yourself right now that you will never allow this to happen again. Your fears directly correlate with why you cannot commit, which correlates to every aspect of your life from a success standpoint. Here are the thought processes that you need to focus on to understand and execute your commitment. First, your livelihood depends on your ability to commit. Second, your maximum potential depends on your level of commitment. Third, your ability to deal with adversity depends on your level of commitment.

Your Livelihood

Very simply put, livelihood is just the ability you have to access things. Time, money, and happiness are all things that can be accessed. In order to obtain, reach, and hold as much of these as possible, you should really accept that your livelihood depends on your ability to commit. Your relationship will never work if you do not pump new energy into it often; in fact, it will wallow away with the wind if you do not create a foundation of commitment. Your husband or wife needs to know that just because you are married now, the work is not over. Understand that you are committed to this relationship 180 percent and that there is no option for you to cheat. The only thing you desire is to keep your partner happy and to grow together. If you are not quite at the married stage, and you are dating someone and there seems to be trust issues causing arguments or petty disagreements, I dare you to try it. Commit to the relationship 180 percent. Let it be known that that is what you are going to do, and then do it. What is the worst outcome? Maybe the relationship does not work out, but at least you can brush your shoulders off knowing you did everything in your power to grow, learn, and support that person. The younger me was full of pride and convinced that he had to be right. Please let go of all childish behaviors because they are preventing you from reaching nirvana, bliss, and happiness. Commit to the person you are spending your time with, and learn more, grow more, and commit more to bettering yourself. I guarantee you the return on your investment will greatly outweigh anything else. The same thing goes for your career. If you do not like going to work, are not earning the amount of income that you desire, or are head over heels in debt, go back to the route question and ask yourself what you deserve. Then commit to it; commit to it 180 percent. When you are 180 percent focused on your income, your finances, and creating wealth, the result can only be what you create. Attract more money, and change the landscape of your financial situation. David Polly, in *The Law of the Garbage Truck*, talks about "dumping" on people and allowing other garbage trucks to "dump on you." First of all, stop dumping on yourself; stop throwing garbage around in your life. Your livelihood matters. Your kids deserve it; your partner deserves it; and you deserve it. Focus on your livelihood by committing yourself 180 percent.

Maximum Potential Reach

At the end of the day, all people want the same thing. We want to fit in to an intrinsic group, and we want to be loved and valued by the people we value and appreciate. Reaching your maximum potential, again, is up to you. Success to you is most likely much different from the way I look at it. Regardless of how we define success, I guarantee you that you are not anywhere near your potential. The potential reach a person has is an analogy for when all cylinders are oiled up, working in tune, and pushing as efficiently as possible. Potential reach is when you have all of your attributes working for you. It's when you believe that no matter what you seek, it will happen. It's when the most important question you will ever ask yourself is, "What Do I Deserve?" This is how you will reach your potential. You will commit 180 percent to your goals, desires, and dreams.

Just making the team is not good enough; make sure that your goals are not basic goals. Although this may be a great accomplishment for most people, think about what separates all-stars from bench players. Is it opportunity, skill, or favoritism? I am confident and willing to bet any amount of money that you think the only difference between the star player and the bench player is the ability to overcommit to the team, their skill, and their goal. Just examine an NBA bench. How often do you see players come off the bench because another player got hurt, and then he or she becomes the star? It happens all the time in sports. But why wasn't that person playing? Starters practice. Kobe Bryant has stayed after basketball games when he had bad shooting nights so that he could practice and get his skill right. Ray Allen is known to shoot two hundred free throws before every game as a warm-up. Floyd May weather may be the best boxer of my day and age, and he trains for hours like most people go to work. I remember seeing an interview on ESPN where it was mentioned that Robert Griffin III would work out for six hours at a time. According to Will Smith, if you and he were in a treadmill competition, the only way he would lose is due to his death.

The concept of commitment is the major difference between living a successful, happy life and any other type of life. Will Smith said it best: "Here is what I believe, and I'm willing to die for it."

Most people will never reach their potential. Most people have no idea how much work ethic is required to obtain any degree of success. However, you know it now. You are aware of it; you know what type of commitment it takes to reach success.

Deal with Adversity

Life happens. Life is not easy, but, dammit, life is exactly what you make of it. I know that unexpected things happen such as death, job loss, and fear. For once in your life, let all of that nonsense go. Trust me when I tell you this: failure does not really exist. Acceleration means you will stop thinking that certain life events are equivalent to failure— because they are not. When your car breaks down in the middle of the road, when your girlfriend comes to tell you that you need to move out, or when you go all out at work just to have your project come up short and be ridiculed by your regional manager, it's OK. You will get pushed, slammed, and you will fall to the ground over and over. However, acceleration means that you cut your losses, wash your hands, and keep moving forward. Philosopher and singer Aaliyah reminds us, "If at first you don't succeed, pick yourself up and try again."

My grandmother told me when I was seventeen, "Life will throw you blows and knock you down, but getting knocked down does not matter. What matters is whether you lie there and take it or get up and stand strong." Failure does not exist; you are not inadequate; and you are not weak or insufficient enough to accomplish this dream you have. You just have to make a choice; you have to commit to the choice. You have to commit 180 percent—not just today but every day. If you ever

113

played a sport, do you remember that last game, quarter, shot, tackle, swing, or pitch? Do you remember the last time you put on the pride of your school or team and took that jersey off? Do you remember the uncertainty, the questions, and the sad feeling that overtook you? Do you remember what it felt like to walk, drive, or ride home and realize that when you wake up tomorrow you are no longer on the roster? Maybe you did not play sports, but I'm sure you've invested time in a relationship that did not work out. Do you remember that feeling of thinking about all the happy moments, the smiles, and the first time you met that person? I know you remember it because these feelings never go away. At the end of life, at the end of effort, and at the end of acceleration, it starts with the same question that it started with. *What do you deserve?* Can you walk away from the team, the job, your spouse, your kids, and your goals every single day knowing you put forth 180 percent of your capacity? Have you committed to doing so well in succeeding and learning that you can walk away knowing your effort was never in question?

See, when life hits you in the face, you have to roll with the punches and recover. You have to catch back up to your goal, your plan, or your dream. Acceleration will only occur when you keep moving forward, regardless of your turbulence, regardless of the conflict and problems. What do you deserve? If you deserve bliss, nirvana, and success, then you are required to commit to every single thing you desire. Nobody will give you what you deserve. You have to create, attract, and design the path for it to flow to you.

If you placed a 4x4 plank on the ground and walked across it, what would happen? It would be a very easy thing to do because walking across this 4x4 is easy. What if you walked across the same 4x4 every morning at six o'clock, and you did it with grace? What happens after a year of doing this behavior? Well, you would probably become an extreme expert at walking across this plank. What happens when you elevate that plank and you sit that plank on top of two ladders that are perpendicular? How about elevated at twelve feet? Would you be able to walk across this plank? At some point, some fear may set in. You may process some things, like falling off and hurting yourself. You may think of the wind coming and pushing the board over, and you falling into the trees. Ask yourself, "What do I deserve?" Let's assume this 4x4 plank represents the road you have to travel every day to create happiness, success, and wealth. Let's assume that plank represents everything you desire. Would you still question walking across that plank? Knowing that, you would walk across the plank and do it quickly.

Let's take it a step further. What if you put that plank over shark-infested waters, at the top of the tallest building in the world, or if you placed it between two helicopters while fighting crosswinds? Remember, the idea here is that this plank is everything you deserve. This is how life works a lot of the time. We get so many things thrown at us, and they distort, cloud, and disrupt us from our main goal. Look at your life right now. I'm sure you've had some crosswinds and turbulence. My suggestion to you? Ask yourself what you deserve. Once you know what you deserve, you will walk across that plank at the speed of light. Your commitment to these plans matter. You will notice that when you are faced with a thought or a decision, when life kicks you in the ass, or when you're torn over what decision to make, you *will* come back to that almighty question. You will understand what you deserve, and you will run across that plank blind if you have to. You will run across that plank naked, with no socks, even if there was oil on the plank. Once you become accelerated, you will see that your commitment is so vast and deep that you never even thought about the circumstances.

18. THE QUESTIONS?

What do you deserve?

What is the most important thing to you?

Are you giving enough love?

Are you adding value to anyone's life?

Are you abusing what you can take from another person?

Are you waking up with bliss everyday? If not – what actions are you going to take to improve your life?

How much longer will you allow opportunity to pass you up?

How much longer will you live with regret?

Do you have a plan in place?

Are you Executing(the how) your plan?

Are you part of *The Accelerated?*

The Accelerated:
Success is A Choice

CPSIA information can be obtained at www.ICGtesting.com
Printed in the USA
BVOW06s0401280716

457093BV00022B/249/P